He gave her a long kiss that sent a deep shudder through her whole frame.

Theresa dropped her bundle to the ground and threw her arms around Philippe. They sank slowly onto her blanket, devouring each other with kisses. The wind rustled gently through the long fronds of the willow trees, swaying them gently to and fro, and a thousand stars looked down upon them.

They looked into each other's eyes as though they wished to memorize the act of love, to crystallize it and carry it with them forever. The thought lay between them, unspoken: this could be the last time.

Afterwards they lay in each other's arms, spent, and fell into a deep sleep of exhaustion and contentment. The last thing Theresa thought, as she drifted off to sleep, was: whatever they do to us, whatever may follow, I will have this to remember.

OUTCASTS FROM EDEN

Katherine Sargent

FAWCETT GOLD MEDAL • NEW YORK

A Fawcett Gold Medal Book

Published by Ballantine Books

Library of Congress Catalog Card Number: 83-90560

ISBN 0-449-12433-9

Manufactured in the United States of America

First Ballantine Books Edition: May 1984

For my husband and favorite Acadian,
Eddie Provost

Ye who believe in affection that hopes, and endures, and is patient,
Ye who believe in the beauty and strength of woman's devotion,
List to the mournful tradition, still sung by the pines of the forest;
List to a tale of Love in Acadie, the home of the happy.

Henry Wadsworth Longfellow, *Evangeline*

Chapter One

From the village of Grand Pré a road ran south, and crossed the Gaspereau River by a narrow bridge that could only be used at low tide. At three o'clock on a September morning, in the year 1755, a solitary horseman traveled north on that road toward the river and village. The rider, a slender, auburn-haired youth, crouched low in the saddle, urging his mount on by talking in his ear and whipping him with the reins. Occasionally, the young man looked over his shoulder for his pursuers, but the road stretched empty behind him, marked only by the shadows of trees cast by the brilliant moonlight. The shadows trembled and shifted as a light wind rustled the leaves. Flecks of foam on the horse's bit and his heaving, sweat-soaked sides indicated that he was near exhaustion.

"We're almost home free! We've done it again!" the young man whispered in a low voice. His mount twitched his ears in response and labored dutifully on. The incoming tide had risen just far enough to cover the bridge's planks, and the horse's pace slowed for an instant before he plunged into the water. His hoofs threw up spray as he ran, but the water was not yet high enough to impede his speed. On the other side of the river, the rider looked over his shoulder once again as his horse scrambled up the bank. Philippe Bernard, for that was the rider's name, threw back his head and laughed. "By the time they get here, the bridge will be completely under water, and before they swim across against the tide, I'll be long gone!"

The horse's hoofs thundered down the road as Philippe whipped his mount to a final burst of speed. A few hundred yards from a large farmhouse, he drew his horse to a halt, slipped lightly from the saddle, and tethered his mount to a tree. "Good boy!" he said, stroking his horse's nose. "You'll have a good rub and a breakfast of oats after I've seen Theresa." The horse whinnied softly and nuzzled Philippe's hand. After giving his mount's neck a final pat, Philippe began slipping noiselessly from tree to tree, emitting a long, low whistle, an imitation of the call of the whippoorwill.

Inside the house, Claire Landry, always a light sleeper, awoke at once and shook the shoulder of the sister whose bed she shared. "Theresa, wake up! It's Philippe!"

Theresa Landry sat up slowly, digging her knuckles into large dark eyes whose lids were swollen with sleep. "Why does he always have to come in the middle of the night?" she grumbled, slowly lifting her nightgown over her mass of dark curly hair. Claire stole an envious sidelong glance at her sister's full breasts.

"You know where he's been—smuggling right under the noses of the British!" Claire giggled. "He gets paid in real gold! I wonder how much he's got now? Better hurry—if you keep the 'Red Fox' waiting, some other girl will grab him!" Claire giggled again.

She's silly, thought Theresa, looking down at her fourteen-year-old sister from the superior height of her sixteen years. Both girls got out of bed, and while Theresa dressed, Claire opened the door and peered out cautiously. She and Theresa shared a small room off the main room of the house where their parents and the younger children slept in a large bed close to the fireplace. The older girls' rooms in Acadian homes were placed so that they could not get outside at night without passing their parents, whereas the older boys slept upstairs in a loft that had its own outside staircase so that they could come in late without disturbing the household. Sons were expected to sow their wild oats, but girls were carefully

2

guarded. It isn't fair, thought Theresa, as she finished buttoning her dress.

"I'll keep an eye on them. You go ahead," Claire whispered. She reached out her hand, detaining her sister. "Tell me what it's like, Theresa. What is it like when Philippe makes love to you?"

"It's better than the very best thing you ever felt. I can't describe it—you'll have to find out for yourself. Go back to sleep," Theresa said impatiently. Keeping an eye on the large bed in the central room, she tiptoed past her family, grateful that her parents were sound sleepers. She stopped once, her heart in her mouth, as little Evariste whimpered in his sleep. The child turned to his other side without waking, and Theresa heaved a sigh of relief as she slipped out the front door and drew a deep breath of the cool night air.

A few moments later, she was inside the barn and in her lover's arms. Without a word, Philippe unbuttoned her dress, pulled it over her head, and tossed it into the hay, then pressed her to him, devouring her with kisses. She removed his shirt and trousers with practiced hands, and they sank into the fragrant hay, piled high after the recent harvest. They made love twice, the first time roughly, with greedy haste, and then more slowly, savoring each other's bodies with lips and hands.

"You haven't said a word," she said at last, sinking back into the hay with a sigh of contentment.

"First things first," Philippe murmured, kissing the hollow of her throat and stroking her sweat-moistened flesh with gentle, expert fingers.

"Everything went well?" she asked as he began kissing her closed eyelids.

"Perfectly. They'll never catch me."

"Sooner or later they will. You'll have to give up smuggling after we're married. It's too risky," she said with mock severity. It was one of the games they played. Theresa pretended to disapprove of Philippe's activities, but he knew she was proud of his skill and daring, as were all the Acadians. Theresa was the envy of all the unmarried girls in the village for having captured the heart of the "Red Fox," who slipped around the British soldiers now occupying their homeland.

"Enough of me," he said, running his hands down the contours of her body. "I'd rather talk about you and the parts of you I love best." He kissed her neck, her breasts, and the backs of her hands. Then he took her foot in his hand and began kissing her toes one by one. "Your toes are like little mushrooms."

"That tickles," Theresa said with a laugh, attempting unsuccessfully to wrest her foot from his grasp. Philippe responded by tickling the soles of her feet until she begged for mercy, with tears of laughter streaming down her face.

"Your feet are cold," he said, relenting at last. He began rubbing them briskly between his hands.

"After we're married, I'll warm them on your legs."

"You'd better not put those lumps of ice on me in the middle of the night!"

"Well, you know the saying—'Cold hands, warm heart.' "

"Yes, but you haven't heard the other half of it—'Cold feet, no sweetheart.' "

Theresa groaned. "That is undoubtedly the worst rhyme I've ever heard." She threw her arms impulsively around his neck. "Oh, Philippe, I miss you so much when we're apart. I'll die if Papa doesn't give in soon and let us get married."

"Marriage can wait. What I want now is some sleep. I've had none tonight and very little last night."

"Then be off with you," she said, pushing him playfully. "You can't sleep here."

"Just for a while," he said. "Stand guard while I catch a quick nap."

"No, Philippe, it's too risky," she said.

"Just for a few minutes," he said, stroking her thighs slowly. She shivered and lay back, opening herself to his touch. The scent of the hay was delicious, and it felt so good to lie in his arms. What bliss it would be for the two of them to sleep in the same bed every night, with the blessing of the law and the church, instead of snatching stolen moments in haystacks! She relaxed in Philippe's arms and decided she would allow herself the luxury of closing her eyes, just for a moment. . . .

Chapter Two

Theresa was pulled slowly from sleep by the sound of the barn door opening. For a moment, she could not remember where she was, and she stared, puzzled, at the first gray light of dawn filtering in through the open door. She peered over the edge of the loft and dimly made out the form of her father, who, as always, was taking care of his livestock before breakfast. Her eyes turned slowly to her sleeping lover. Now fully awake, she tried in vain to suppress a quick surge of panic.

"Philippe!" she whispered, shaking his shoulder. "Wake up! It's my father!" Gaspard Landry would kill them both if he found them naked in the hay. Philippe rolled over, pressing his body to hers, and fitted his hands to the contours of her breasts.

"*Chère*," he murmured, kissing the small hollow at the base of her throat and running the tip of his tongue along her neck. It had never failed to drive her wild before, but now fear of being caught with the man she had been forbidden to see completely conquered desire.

Her father's footsteps paused, as if he were listening, then changed direction and began moving toward the hayloft. At last realizing their predicament, Theresa's lover leaped to his feet and with astonishing haste began dressing. Even as she was pulling down her skirt and buttoning her bodice, Theresa looked at Philippe's naked form from head to toe and thought once again that she had never seen such a beautiful body. Philippe Bernard was of medium height, narrow waisted and straight hipped, and deceptively lean. It was not until he had lifted her effortlessly from the floor at the Leleux' dance, on that night last March when she had first taken serious notice of him, that Theresa realized what strength lay in those slender limbs. Nor, she thought, was there a handsomer face in Grand Pré. Philippe had deep brown eyes, auburn hair burned red by the sun, and features so finely chiseled one would have been tempted to call them delicate were it not for the aggressiveness of his bearing. But Theresa was incapable of objectivity when it came to Philippe Bernard.

Her father's footsteps were now on the ladder leading up to the hayloft, each rung creaking under his tread. There was no avenue of escape. Philippe began pulling bits of hay from Theresa's curly black hair and gave her a smile and a wink of reassurance. She felt as if her limbs had turned to water. Was Philippe afraid of nothing?

Her father's gray head appeared over the top of the ladder, and he took in the situation at a glance. His eyes turned to steel. "Get out," he said in a quiet voice to Philippe.

"Please, sir, don't blame Theresa. The responsibility is mine."

"Get out before I kill you." Theresa shuddered. Her father sometimes spoke in mock anger to his family, in a deep, hollow voice accompanied by a bit of a swagger. No one took him seriously when he spoke that way, but on the rare occasions when he was really angry, he would speak very quietly, the way he was now, and woe betide the person who did not heed him then.

"You'd better go," she said meekly to Philippe. As soon as Gaspard Landry climbed into the loft and sat down beside his daughter, Philippe ran lightly down the ladder and out into the early morning.

Gaspard Landry sat in silence, his face stricken. The last time Theresa had seen that look on her father's face was the night he received word that his daughter Isabelle had died giving birth to her first child. Theresa would have preferred shouts and threats, even a beating, to that dreadful silence. When she could bear it no longer, she said, "Philippe would have been long gone, but we fell asleep."

"It's a good thing for me I found out now instead of later. How long has this been going on?"

"Only for a few months, since you denied us permission to marry." —

"Are you pregnant?"

"No, Papa." Theresa flushed and looked away.

Her father buried his face in his hands. Suddenly, he looked old, crumpled, defeated. It seemed to Theresa that he had somehow collapsed, turning into an old man as she looked at him. "How could you do such a thing to us?" he said at last.

"You wouldn't listen, Papa. We should have been married by now instead of sneaking around in barns."

"Oh, Lord, child, you're too young to marry anyone, let alone the likes of Philippe Bernard."

"Cecile Babineaux married when she was only fourteen, and so did Amelia Trahan."

"But they weren't my baby."

"I'm not your baby, either, Papa. You've got to accept the fact that I'm a grown woman."

"A woman." Gaspard shook his head. "No, Theresa, you're not a woman. You're a spoiled, willful child. Perhaps it's my fault for not being stricter with you. I never could deny you anything you had your heart set on."

"Then don't deny me Philippe. Oh, Papa, I love him so much, more than anything on earth. I'll never love anyone else the way I love him. If your objections made any sense, I'd listen to them, but they don't. You pretend to disapprove of his smuggling, but I know you secretly admire him. Everyone does. Why should half of what we own go to the British?"

She turned her large dark eyes on her father with a look of such desperate pleading that he had to turn away. Gaspard Landry loved all of his children, and he attempted to be impartial, but he knew that he would always love Theresa best. It was not only that she was the prettiest of his daughters. She was gay and affectionate and warmhearted, with an infectious laugh that seemed to bubble up from inside like water from a spring, and she had a sunny nature that no misfortune could repress for long. But for all her love of fun, she was not irresponsible. She was a hard worker, a great help with the younger children, and she frequently anticipated her mother's needs by performing household tasks without being asked. Although she could occasionally be stubborn when denied something she wanted, she had for the most part been an obedient child who had given her parents little trouble. She had never before defied Gaspard, and he was so shocked that she had formed a sexual liaison behind his back, against his express command that she cease seeing Philippe Bernard, that he was at a loss as to how the situation should be handled. He sensed a bedrock of resistance beneath her amiable exterior, and he had to risk the danger that too much harshness on his part could force her into even more flagrant defiance.

He tried to steer a middle course between reason and the exercise of parental authority. "It's not just the smuggling that I disapprove of. I've been a judge of men long enough to know that Philippe Bernard has a wild, crazy streak. I don't think he's reliable. I know that he's handsome, and his nocturnal heroics have half the girls in the village chasing him, but the qualities you look for in a man when you're young and the ones you learn to value later aren't the same. You may think that he's exciting now, but you'll think differently when you've got a houseful of children."

"Philippe loves me. He would never do anything to hurt me."

"Perhaps not intentionally. I know his type. He'll behave badly, and then charm you when you get angry over it, and then he'll behave badly again, until one day your anger is too deep to be charmed away. I won't be around forever to take care of you. You're from one of the richest and most highly respected families in Grand Pré, Theresa, and I can't sit idly by and watch you throw yourself away. What do you think I've worked so hard for, if not to provide my children with a good life and a secure future?"

"You just don't want to let me go, and you're making up excuses to keep me from marrying."

8

Gaspard knew that there was some truth in what she said. Theresa had blossomed physically at a very early age, earlier than his other daughters, and he knew that he was staving off the day when he would have to part with her. How had she grown up so fast? It seemed only yesterday that she had sat on his knee, cooing and gurgling and clutching at his nose and cheeks with dimpled baby fingers. The thought of those hands on a man's naked body, bold and eager, filled him with an uneasy rage that he tried in vain to suppress. If he must give her up, at least let it be to someone he trusted.

"I'll not deny that it will be a sad day for me when I part with you, but that's not the point. A girl as pretty as you, with your connections, can have anyone you like if you'll just be a little patient. You know my Cousin Charles's son Leon is interested in you, and if he'd ask for you tomorrow, I'd give you my blessing."

"Cousin Leon! Please don't start on Cousin Leon again! He's so dull I want to go to sleep just listening to him talk!"

"He's steady and reliable and will make some girl a wonderful husband."

"You've never felt about anyone the way I feel about Philippe, or you wouldn't talk this way."

"I have felt about someone the way you feel about Philippe, and I know from bitter experience exactly what I'm talking about. I know what you think of me. You think I'm a doddering old graybeard who hasn't the faintest idea what it means to be young and in love."

Theresa felt a rush of blood to her cheeks. That was exactly what she thought, but she would never have said so to her father, and she was surprised that he had read her mind so easily.

Gaspard put his arm around his daughter and paused a moment, considering. "Theresa, I'm going to tell you something I've never talked to anyone about. Your mother, as you know, is my second wife. I don't believe in speaking ill of the dead, especially not the mother of my children, but I think I should tell you the story of my first marriage. When I was eighteen years old, I married Rosalie Comeaux. She was the prettiest girl in Grand Pré, and the best dancer. My parents were opposed to the match. They told me that she was lazy and unstable and good for little beyond dancing and flirtation, but I was mad about her, and I thought I was the luckiest man in the world when she accepted me.

"We were happy for the first year, even though she was a terrible cook and an indifferent housekeeper, and jealous of anything that took my attention away from her. Then the babies started coming. It didn't bother me so much when she neglected me, but when she neglected our children, that was another matter entirely. Every time she had a baby, I thought: she's going to love this one. This time she's going to change. After my family and her family scolded her long enough, she started keeping the children clean and became a better housekeeper, but she was only fulfilling an irksome duty. It never occurred to her to pick up her babies, to fondle them, to hold them. She lived for escapes—for dancing or gossiping with the other wives or just for getting out of the house whenever she could.

"When our son Sosthène was sick with the smallpox, the LeBlancs gave a dance, and Rosalie insisted on going. I told her that we should stay at home with the baby, but she pouted and insisted on going. Five days later, Sosthène died. I know now that he would probably have died, anyway, but at the time I turned on Rosalie and accused her of killing him by her neglect. After that, she became silent and withdrawn, and she started eating too much. Nothing pleased her or made her happy. She never laughed or sang about the house the way she used to, and she would burst into tears for no reason at all. That's all she did—eat and cry, eat and cry. She got fat, and then she wouldn't even go to dances anymore, because she was no longer the prettiest girl in Grand Pré. She complained constantly of being tired, even when our oldest daughter took over most of the housework.

"I hate to admit this, but when she died, it was a blessing to the whole family. I had to marry again soon, with such a large brood of children at home, but you can be sure that the second time around I picked a sensible woman who knew how to make a good home and loved children. Your mother and I have been very happy together, even though I didn't have the feeling for her that I had for Rosalie in the beginning. I married Marie-Jeanne with my head instead of my heart, but over the years we've grown like two plants that have been grafted together, and now I'd be intolerably lonely without her."

Theresa digested all of this in silence. She was flattered that her father was confiding in her and pleased that for the first time in her life he was talking to her as one adult to another. Still, she refused to be swayed. "You can't judge the whole world by one bad experience. Besides, you admitted yourself that your parents couldn't talk you out of marrying Rosalie Comeaux. She may have been the wrong girl for you, but you had to find that out for yourself."

"I just don't want you to repeat my mistakes."

"I'm not going to repeat your mistakes. I'm going to make my own. I'd rather take a chance with Philippe than get stuck with someone dull and boring like Cousin Leon. What kind of pleasure would I get from life with a man like him?" She thought of going to bed with her Cousin Leon, and somehow the image of the two of them together made her think of sinking slowly to the bottom of a muddy pond.

"This isn't the only pleasure in life," said Gaspard with a wave toward the depression Philippe's body had made in the hay. "That pales after a while. You'll have pleasure in your family. I don't just mean your children. Your aunts and uncles and cousins and in-laws are all your family. You're related to half of the people in Grand Pré, and they're all a part of your family. And you'll have the land."

What strange notions her father had! thought Theresa. As if she could ever grow tired of making love to Philippe! "Land, pooh! Who ever heard of taking pleasure from land! Land is just dirt!"

"Never let me hear you say that again, Theresa. Our ancestors found a wilderness here, and they struggled to turn it into a home. Don't you ever forget it. Come down now."

It was fully light outside the barn, and Gaspard Landry led his daughter out into the new day. With a broad sweep of his arm, he indicated the landscape before them. It was a beautiful sight, and the way Grand Pré looked at that moment was to be indelibly printed on Theresa's memory. The sun was rising in a brilliant blue autumn sky. From every chimney, the smoke from breakfast fires curled lazily, its pungent odor mingling pleasantly with the smells of stubbled wheat fields and rich earth. To the southeast, a clump of houses at the center of Grand Pré lay clustered on gentle slopes, and to the east and west a continuous line of dwellings stretched out from the village. To the north lay the rich, rolling meadows on which grew the grain that made the area the breadbasket of Acadia. Even farther to the north lay the shimmering waters of the Minas Basin. The road in front of their house led south to the Gaspereau River.

"This is your heritage," Gaspard Landry said to his daughter. "This land belongs to you and your children and your children's children."

"It doesn't belong to us anymore. It belongs to the English. They don't even call it Acadia. Now it's Nova Scotia."

"The English may call it anything they like, but it's still Acadia, and it always will be. In the war France and England are fighting now, or in the next one, Acadia will be ceded back to the French, and our descendants will be here long after the English have left."

They were strolling slowly toward the Landry home. "Will you finish getting the wheat in today?" Theresa asked in an attempt to change the subject.

"No. It will probably take us two more days. We could have finished today if it weren't for that silly business at the church this afternoon. John Winslow will no doubt make the most of an opportunity to strut and pose and take two hours to read a proclamation that anyone else could read in ten minutes."

All of the men in Grand Pré above the age of fourteen had been ordered to appear at the Church of St. Charles at three o'clock to hear a proclamation from the English governor read by Col. John Winslow.

"What is the proclamation about?"

"Who knows? Just the latest piece of nonsense from His Excellency Governor Lawrence in Halifax," said Gaspard, his voice heavy with sarcasm. "We'll go in for breakfast together as if nothing has happened," he added in a low voice as they reached the door. "No one must say a word to your mother about this business between you and Philippe. It would break her heart."

"I still want to marry Philippe, Papa."

Gaspard sighed. "I'll strike a bargain with you. Wait for a year, and if you still feel the same way next harvest season, I'll give my permission. But there'll be no more sneaking around in barns."

"A year? A whole year?" Theresa felt as though her father had asked her to wait for a lifetime.

"A year isn't such a long time. If you were as old as you seem to think you are, you'd know that."

Chapter Three

*Shortly before three o'clock that afternoon, the Church of St.
Charles began to fill slowly with men and boys.* Those who
arrived early greeted each other and stood in small groups
outside, talking to each other of crops and the weather. When
Gaspard Landry spotted Philippe Bernard, he stiffened and
gave him a curt nod. Then he turned abruptly to hail his
cousin Charles, and the two men and their sons entered
together. Once inside, the men waited silently, tanned, work-
worn hands stretched out stiffly on the knees of their pants,
dark eyes fixed straight ahead.

Col. John Winslow stood looking out of a window of the
priest's home, which he had requisitioned for his private use,
and watched as the men filed quietly into the church. He
shook his head and sighed. If he lived among these people for
a lifetime, he would never understand them, and he was glad
that he would soon be rid of them forever. Since Acadia had
been ceded to the English in 1713 under the terms of the
Treaty of Utrecht and renamed Nova Scotia by the British, the
French inhabitants of the province had been described as
"ungovernable" and "insubordinate" by the provincial
administrators. It was not so much that they were openly
rebellious. If that had been the case, they would have been

easier to cope with. The insubordination of the Acadians was more subtle, indirect. They were fiercely independent people who refused to show proper deference toward those in command, and they had no real respect for rank or authority. Although most of their ancestors, who had emigrated from western France early in the seventeenth century, had been the humblest of farmers, the Acadians had prospered in their new home and adopted the New World attitude that they were as good as any man alive. They had never borne arms against the English or sided with France in her interminable wars with England—indeed, they hardly seemed to be tied to their mother country at all except by language and religion—but they had still repeatedly refused to take an unconditional oath of loyalty to the English crown.

The Acadians undermined English authority in other ways, as well. For years they had cheated the English of a portion of wheat, cattle, and produce, all of which were taxed to feed the soldiers at the English garrisons. The excuses were always the same:

"My wheat crop failed."

"There wasn't enough rain, and the fruit in my orchards withered on the trees."

"My hens aren't laying."

"My cattle got sick and died."

The English knew that they were lying, but it was hard to prove it. One couldn't set watchdogs over them day and night. The Acadians took the cattle and produce that should have gone to the English and smuggled it to Boston merchants at Baie Verte or to the French fortress of Louisburg on Cape Breton Island. There they sold it, realizing a tidy profit, while English soldiers lived on lean rations.

The cleverest of the smugglers was that young rogue, Philippe Bernard, the man the Acadians called the "Red Fox." Winslow laughed ruefully. The name was apt. What was the word the Acadians used to describe someone who was crafty and clever? *Canaille*, that was it. The word suited Philippe Bernard perfectly. He was *canaille*, like a sly red fox. Philippe Bernard knew the Acadian countryside as well as he knew the back of his hand, and he had cultivated friends

15

among the Micmac Indians, who helped shelter him when he slipped around the British sentries. Everyone knew what he was doing, but no one had been clever enough to catch him at it. At last, even Winslow's own men had come to have a grudging respect for the wily young Frenchman. He was only eighteen years old, but he had been a thorn in Winslow's side for years.

The previous week, Philippe Bernard had walked past Colonel Winslow in front of the blacksmith's shop with the slow, swaggering gait Winslow detested so, and instead of bowing civilly, as it behooved him to do in the presence of his betters, Bernard had given Winslow a most impertinent grin and strutted past as if it were he, and not Winslow, who was master there. There had been witnesses to the humiliating incident, Acadian men whose dark eyes had mocked Winslow and who hid their laughter behind their hands. Remembering, Winslow clenched his fists and felt his face burn crimson with rage. He had vowed to see that insolent scoundrel Philippe Bernard defeated if it were the last thing he did, and his moment of triumph was about to arrive.

Winslow had a few minutes left; there was no need to hurry. He turned away from the window and examined himself in the full-length mirror he had brought with him. In the glass, he saw a stout man of fifty-four with a round red face, double chin, and high arched eyebrows that gave his face a look of perpetual astonishment. He was fond of finery, and his scarlet uniform was laden with gold braid and lace. A powdered wig, curled to perfection and tied at the nape of his neck with a black ribbon, completed his costume. The soldier surveyed himself from head to toe, patted his wig, and turned back to the window, satisfied that he looked his best.

Winslow was a man of humble origins who had risen through the ranks by hard work and perseverance. The church and the army offered the only avenues of advancement for a poor boy, and as he had no religious leanings, he had chosen a military career. The Acadians seemed to find his drive to improve himself absurd, even as he found their lack of ambition incomprehensible. A few of them had amassed considerable wealth, but most of them were no more industrious than necessary to provide for themselves and their families. They were for the most part content with elementary learning. They had a great love of music, dancing, and other harmless forms of entertainment, and seemed content to live out their lives within the bosoms of their families.

Their families! He gave a snort of laughter. God, how these people could breed! He had never seen folk to match them for the production of children. Even with a high infant mortality rate, it was not unusual to find families with fifteen or even twenty children. Since second cousins could legally marry, a man's great-grandchildren often married each other, leading to such a tangled web of family relationships that he wondered if the Acadians themselves could straighten out all the ways in which they were related to each other. Often, whole villages would be comprised of a single extended family clan. It would have been easier to contend with them if there had not been more and more of them every year.

That brought one to the real problem: what, ultimately, was to be done with such a large body of French Catholics in a Protestant province? The idea of deportation had been suggested by several governors over the years, but it seemed a drastic measure, expensive and impractical, not to mention cruel and unnecessary, unless the Acadians represented a serious threat. Since they took so little interest in European politics, it seemed unlikely that they would ever actually rebel against English rule.

Winslow himself had feared the impact on the land of Nova Scotia should deportation come about. Until there were enough English immigrants to replace them, farms would be left destitute and revert to a primitive state without the Acadians to cultivate them. The northern part of Grand Pré had been a marsh when the Acadians had moved there from the first French settlement at Port Royal. Winslow had to give them credit for one thing—they had devised a damned clever system of dikes to hold back the sea. It required great skill to put down a sluice in the bed of the river channel to let out the fresh water from within and at the same time to keep out the salt water from the rapid tides. It had taken three years after the first dikes were built for the rain to wash the soil free of salt so that it could be planted, but after that, the land had proved amazingly fertile and ideal for the cultivation of wheat. The dikes required constant repair and supervision, and without someone to maintain them, the land would once again be reclaimed by the sea.

The issue that finally brought matters to a head was the outbreak of the French and Indian War. General Braddock's defeat at the Battle of the Wilderness on July twenty-third, 1755, had heightened English fear of the French inhabitants of Nova Scotia, and after a last futile appeal to the Acadians to swear loyalty to England, Governor Lawrence had decided to deport them to the thirteen English colonies, splitting them up into small groups so as to diffuse the threat of a large mass of potentially hostile French Catholics in the New World. To ensure that the Acadians would not attempt to regroup in the colonies, no ship was to know the destination of any other. At the most important military posts throughout Acadia—Beaubassin, Pisiquid, Fort Beausejour, Port Royal, Grand Pré—the adult Acadian males were to be lured into their respective posts under the pretext of hearing a proclamation from the governor and would there be forcibly detained until the arrival of sufficient transport to carry them to the colonies. It was Colonel Winslow's duty to execute the deportation of the citizens of Grand Pré.

Since there were far more adult Acadian men than there were English soldiers, it was imperative that the English have the advantage of surprise. Standing at the window, Winslow scrutinized the Acadians anxiously to see if he could detect any signs of fear or suspicion. The men had been summoned to hear proclamations read before; there was no reason for them to think that this occasion would be any different from the others. Winslow was satisfied that the Acadians showed no apprehension toward the redcoats who surrounded them.

At precisely three o'clock, Colonel Winslow traveled the short distance from the priest's home to the church, accompanied by a strong escort; once inside, he looked at the rows of dark eyes that regarded him in expectant silence. Then, lowering his eyes, Winslow read a proclamation that was translated into French by an interpreter, the gist of which was that the

18

land, property, and livestock of the Acadians were now forfeit to the crown. Furthermore, as soon as there were enough
ships in the Minas Basin to transport them, they were to be
deported to a destination that Winslow was not at liberty to
divulge. The Acadians were to be given liberty to carry as
much money and as many of their household goods as they
could without overcrowding the vessels in which they would
travel. Winslow assured the men that he would do everything
in his power to protect the goods of the Acadians and to see
to it that whole families were put on the same vessel.

He concluded by saying; "I must also inform you that it is
His Majesty's pleasure that you remain in security under the
inspection and direction of the troops that I have the honor to
command until such time as you shall be deported." Winslow
informed the astounded Acadians that they were to remain
prisoners of the king in the Church of St. Charles until their
departure and that as all their horses, cattle, sheep, goats,
hogs, and poultry had been declared forfeit to the crown, no
one was to hurt, kill, or destroy any of the above possessions
or rob their own orchards and gardens.

For a few moments after he had finished reading the
proclamation, a deathly silence fell over the church. Men
turned to look at each other, puzzled, incredulous, dumbfounded.
Winslow had succeeded in taking the men of Grand Pré
completely by surprise. It was the harvest season, and after
hearing the proclamation, the Acadians, to a man, had expected to return to their fields to work during the remaining
daylight hours.

Philippe Bernard was the first to grasp the full import of
the message. While Winslow had been reading the proclamation, Philippe began to recall, suddenly, small disturbances in
the areas he had visited—unusual reticence on the part of the
Micmac Indians; strange rumors that had trickled down from
Fort Beausejour, which the English had taken over and renamed Fort Cumberland; unwonted movements of English
troops and reinforcements at the major posts. Yes, of course,
now it all made sense. At the time, he had been too preoccu-
pied with his own affairs to put the clues together. It seemed
incomprehensible to him, as indeed it did to all the Acadians,

19

that the English would ever actually deport them, so he had brushed the small warning signs aside until it was too late. What a fool he had been!

With a shout, Philippe leaped from his pew, followed by a few of the younger men, and tried to force the door of the church, only to be driven back by the muskets of the soldiers standing guard. A soldier grasped Philippe firmly by the arm and returned him to his pew. A low murmur broke out among the men, swelling to a loud clamor, as each man turned to his neighbor for assurance that he had heard correctly.

Colonel Winslow pounded his fist on the pulpit. "Order, I say! Silence!" The roar of voices subsided. Gaspard Landry, one of the few Acadians who could speak English, raised his hand. "What have we done to deserve deportation?" Landry asked. "We have never borne arms against England or sided with France in her wars with England."

"It is not my place to justify such decisions, only to carry them out. I cannot argue the justice of the command, which has been handed down from Governor Lawrence. All I can say is that you were given repeated opportunities to take an unconditional oath of loyalty to the English crown, which you obstinately refused to do. Now that England is once again at war with France, there can be no such thing as neutrality. If you are not on our side, you are on the side of our enemy, France."

"Do these orders come from England?"

"I take my orders from Governor Lawrence. It is not my place to question his source."

Gaspard translated his questions and answers to his countrymen, who were gasping and shaking their heads. "Where are we to be taken?" Landry asked Winslow.

"As the proclamation states, I am not at liberty to divulge that information," Colonel Winslow replied stiffly. Gaspard translated his question and Winslow's answer for the others. The men roared in protest.

"Will we all be relocated in the same place?" Landry asked.

"I am sorry, I cannot give you any information concerning your destination," came the reply.

20

"But you said that families would not be separated from each other," Landry persisted. "I myself am directly related to half of the inhabitants of Grand Pré."

"By families I mean spouses and dependent children under the age of twelve," said Winslow. "I cannot assure that you will remain with all of your relatives." This information, when translated, produced another roar of protest. Once again, Colonel Winslow pounded his fist to restore order.

"When will we leave?" was Landry's next question.

"As soon as we have enough ships to transport you," came the reply. "It will not be long, I assure you."

"And you actually intend to keep us locked up here in the church until you forcibly eject us and our families from our homes?" The Acadians looked about. They were suddenly aware that the church and stockade were bristling with armed redcoats. The Acadians had no weapons at all—nothing, in fact, but the clothes they wore.

"Yes, there must be no possibility of insurrection."

"But what of our families? Who is to inform them and protect them in our absence?"

Colonel Winslow considered. "I will release twenty men to return to their homes and assure all families that you are safe and well treated and to help prepare for your leave-taking. Your families will be safe under the protection of the men under my command."

Gaspard Landry had one more question. "Are we not to be compensated in any way for our property? We reclaimed this land from the sea. How can you justify stealing it from us?"

"The value of your lands will be used to defray the cost of your relocation," said Colonel Winslow. "You may decide among yourselves which twenty men are to be released," he said. With that, he turned and walked from the church without looking back, his body held rigidly erect.

Once inside the priest's house, he sank into a chair and mopped his brow with a lace handkerchief. He knew that the Acadians had done nothing to deserve deportation, and the sight of their stricken, incredulous faces had made him feel guiltier than he liked to admit. Still, he smiled with grim satisfaction as he recalled Philippe Bernard's panicked reaction. His revenge could not have been more effective.

Inside the church, the leaders of the Acadians called a hasty conference. After an hour of debate, twenty men, Gaspard Landry among them, were selected and released to bear their dreadful intelligence to the community.

Chapter Four

Gaspard Landry trudged dejectedly toward his home, rehearsing in his mind various ways to break the bad news to his family. As he approached, he saw Theresa sitting under the willow tree in front of the Landry house, amusing the two youngest children, Evariste and Richard. His wife and Claire were preparing supper. For the first time in years, there would be only six people at the supper table, as his and Marie-Jeanne's oldest sons, René and Claude, were locked up in the church. His children from his marriage to Rosalie Comeaux were all married and had children of their own. Claude was courting Dora LeBlanc, and everyone expected him to marry her soon. Except for an occasional evening when Claude ate dinner at the LeBlancs', since the birth of baby Richard there had always been the eight of them at table. Already Gaspard could feel the gaps in his family circle.

"Papa!" Theresa called out when she spotted her father. "Where are the boys?"

"They're still in the church," he replied. Theresa shrugged her shoulders and turned back to the string game she was playing with her brothers. Gaspard thought, with a wrench of the heart, that although she had the body of a woman, Theresa's face, with its full mouth and large dark eyes, still had the round, unlined softness of childhood. She had accepted his statement without question.

Inside, Claire was setting the supper table, and Marie-Jeanne was simultaneously bending over her supper pots and listening to a steady stream of chatter from the widow Julia Laperousse, the biggest gossip in the neighborhood, who was holding up a dress to her ample frame.

"I just dropped over to show Marie-Jeanne the dress I made for Clementine to wear to the Oubres' dance next week," she said, pirouetting this way and that. To a green skirt she had attached a bright red bodice. "Clementine can wear almost any color. She is the nicest girl," Julia exclaimed.

Gaspard thought with wry amusement that the surest way to spread information all over Grand Pré had been dropped right in his lap, in the buxom form of Julia Laperousse. He was amazed that he could laugh even at a time like this, but he still could not quite believe that he was to be deprived of all his property and see his family scattered to the four winds. He had been unable to think of a diplomatic way to break the news and in the end came out with it directly. "There may not be a dance at the Oubres' next week," he said. "John Winslow has just informed us that we're to be deported."

Marie-Jeanne pulled her face, red from the supper fire, out from her pots. "Deported?" she said dully. "Deported where?"

"He refused to tell us. He says that our property is to be confiscated, except for those of our household goods which can be put on the ships, and that we're to be sent away."

"But why?" asked Julia Laperousse, letting Clementine's dress fall over one arm. "Whatever have we done to the English except keep them from robbing us blind?"

"Apparently this is their reprisal for our refusal to sign an oath of loyalty to England."

"But you've been refusing to sign that oath for years," said Marie-Jeanne.

"The new war between France and England has triggered this," her husband replied, sitting down heavily in his chair by the hearth. "Winslow says there can no longer be any such thing as neutrality and that if we are not loyal to England, then we are her foes."

24

The Widow Laperousse, whose mouth was gaping open with shock, now closed it and spoke again. "But that's nonsense! You don't believe him, do you? It must be some sort of trick."

"I've thought of that. There's an outside possibility that this is merely a means of forcing our hand, of making us sign the oath."

"But you don't believe that, do you?" his wife asked quietly.

"No, my dear, I'm afraid not. I think the English are in earnest."

"I can't believe it," said Julia. "There are only five English ships in the harbor, and my family alone would fill one of them!"

"He says that parents and children under the age of twelve are to be kept together, but beyond that, no attempt will be made to see that families remain united."

"That's the most outrageous thing I've ever heard!" Marie-Jeanne raged. Her face had gone a sickly white, and she did not take her stricken eyes off her husband's face. "Where are the boys?" she whispered at last.

"Claude and René and the other men are still at the church. Winslow says that we're to be kept there until there are enough ships in the bay to deport us, to remove the possibility of an insurrection. He let twenty men go to spread the news, but we have to be back at first light tomorrow, or reprisals will be taken against our families."

While the conversation had been in progress, Theresa had slipped quietly into the house with the two boys. "Is Philippe in the church?"

Her father stiffened. "Yes," he replied.

"Oh, Theresa, I thought you'd forgotten him," Marie-Jeanne said. She did not share her husband's dislike of the Bernard boy, but she accepted Gaspard's authority and assumed that Theresa had dismissed him from her mind.

"Well!" sputtered Julia. "Wait till Laura and Clothilde hear about this! I must be going, Marie-Jeanne," she said, bending over and planting a kiss on her neighbor's cheek. "Don't take on so. I'm sure they can't be in earnest!" And with that she scurried through the front door as fast as her feet would carry her, on fire with eagerness to be the first to spread the news.

The evening meal was a silent one in spite of the fact that Marie-Jeanne had prepared all of her husband's favorite foods: beefsteak and potatoes, plenty of bread with fresh apple butter, green beans, and cherry cobbler for dessert. In her youthful ignorance, Theresa's thoughts were all of Philippe: if they were deported and she and Philippe contrived to stay together, they could get married right away without having to wait a year for her father's consent.

After dinner, Gaspard and Marie-Jeanne moved to their chairs before the hearth with their children around them. After a strained silence, Marie-Jeanne said in a low voice, "It's true, isn't it? They really are going to deport us."

"I'm afraid so, dear," her husband said gently.

Marie-Jeanne buried her face in her hands and began weeping. "Whatever shall we do? Where shall we go?"

Her husband reached over and patted her shoulder clumsily. "I don't know, but we must remain calm for the sake of the children."

"How can we remain calm when we're losing our home and our children?"

"It might not be as bad as all that. We'll be allowed to take with us as much of our property as we can carry. I suggest that you begin collecting your most valuable possessions and put them in the hay wagon. I don't know how much we'll be allowed to take on board. It depends on how crowded the ships are. As for the children, I'll find a way to keep us together. Don't fret."

"I still can't believe it. I keep thinking that tomorrow I'll wake up and life will go on as usual and this will all have been a bad dream." She looked around at the home she had known and loved for twenty years. Like all Acadian farmhouses, the Landry home was dominated by a central room with a stone fireplace large enough for roasting the side of a calf or a whole pig. The spinning wheel held a position of prominence before the fire, while inside the fireplace hung Madame Landry's cooking pots, scrubbed to gleaming perfection. Close enough to the fire to receive its warmth in the freezing Acadian winters was the bed on which she had borne seven children, and behind the bed was the armoire her great-great-great-grandmother had brought with her when she came from Poitou in France. All of the objects she saw were familiar, well-worn, loved. The firelight flickered softly on the walls of her home, which exuded peace and security. How could this all evaporate before her very eyes?

"When will we leave? Where are they taking us?"

"It won't be long now, and no one knows where we're going."

"Will we be given land when we are relocated?"

"I don't know. It would only seem equitable, but no mention has been made of it."

"Will they take us all to the same place?"

"What would be the point of relocating us all in the same place? My guess is that they will break us up into small groups and scatter us about. If we're not too far apart, we'll simply have to get back together somehow." He sighed. "I'm too old to start over again. I've put too much work into this place, but who can challenge the will of God? And please don't worry about Theresa and Claire. I understand the edict mainly refers to young boys under twelve. The girls will be safe with us."

"The cursed English! I'll hate them till the day I die. What have we done to deserve such treatment?"

Gaspard leaned over and put his arm around his wife. She leaned her head on his shoulder. "I don't know. I can't answer your question. But I was just thinking of all the storms the two of us have weathered together—the years the crops failed, the year half our livestock sickened and died. We can survive anything as long as we have each other."

"If only we had the priest to turn to for advice!" cried Marie-Jeanne. "He could tell us what to do." When Colonel Winslow took over the priest's home, he had taken Father Menard prisoner and sent him under armed escort to Fort Edwards.

"We can pray ourselves," said Gaspard. "You don't have to have a priest to pray."

"Yes, surely God will help us. He will listen to our prayers."

Gaspard Landry gathered his children around him, and

27

Theresa, her younger brothers and sister, and her parents said their rosaries before they turned in for the night. The next morning, Gaspard arose before dawn, embraced his wife and each of his children, and returned to the church with a heavy heart.

By then, word of what had transpired in the church had spread throughout the village. The women of Grand Pré, most of whom had never been more than ten miles from home, found deportation almost impossible to comprehend. Still, their homes were barren and silent without their men, and as the days wore on, a pall of gloom, of apprehensive anticipation, hung over the women as they went about their daily tasks. As time passed and their men did not return, the realization that the English were in earnest slowly dawned on them.

Marie-Jeanne Landry threw herself into a frenzy of activity, trying to push away her fears with work, but she had difficulty sleeping. In her twenty years of marriage to Gaspard Landry, she had never before slept without him, and she was haunted by strange dreams. She would wake in the middle of the night clutching her rosary and say a few beads before she slipped back into an uneasy rest. Even when her sleep was uninterrupted, she would wake up tired, unrefreshed.

In addition to their customary duties, the women were now required to provide food for the men in the church. Every day Theresa volunteered to carry food to her father and two older brothers in the hopes of catching a glimpse of Philippe, but the food was always taken at the gate by soldiers. The men were not allowed to loiter near the gate to visit or even catch a glimpse of their female relatives. Theresa comprehended the situation, and her major concern was to see that she and Philippe were not separated when the deportation took place.

For several days, Colonel Winslow paced the floor of the priest's home in an agony of impatience. He had been promised enough ships to transport all the Acadians living in and around Grand Pré—all four thousand of them—but so far there were only five English vessels in the bay. Governor Lawrence had instructed Winslow that no more than two Acadians per ton were to be placed on each ship to avoid overcrowding. The English transports, which had been brought from Boston, were small merchant vessels of from one hundred to one hundred and fifty tons each. At most, he figured that there was room on board the five vessels for twelve hundred and fifty of his deportees. Even with some overcrowding, he would need at least sixteen ships for them all.

Finally, Colonel Winslow decided to load fifty young Acadian men on each of the five vessels waiting in the harbor to reduce the danger of an uprising in the church. To this end, he summoned Gaspard Landry to the priest's home and presented him with a list of the men Winslow had selected for boarding, as he thought it best that the news be conveyed to the Acadians by one of their own. Gaspard scanned the list rapidly. Philippe Bernard's name was on it. Just as Theresa was determined not to be parted from her lover, her father was hoping that he could contrive to separate them. Claude and René were on the list, as well as two of his older married sons. He found it difficult to restrain his tears when he saw that his sons were being torn from him.

"Have we any assurance of being loaded onto the same ships as our sons?" He forced himself to hold his voice steady.

"I have already explained that the utmost effort will be expended to see that parents remain with their younger children. Beyond that, I can make no promises."

"Then what you're saying is that four of my sons are being taken from me, and I may never see them again."

"You're wasting my time, Landry. We must get these men to the ships before the tide turns."

"And I'm to be the Judas who leads them."

"Your duty is to convey the list to your men and explain the situation. My men will do the rest."

Landry gave Winslow a level, penetrating stare. "You'll roast in hell for this." He turned on his heel and brushed past the soldiers who stood in the doorway.

When Gaspard Landry conveyed Colonel Winslow's order to the Acadians, pandemonium broke out. That the English actually meant to separate father from son and brother from brother was incomprehensible to men who could not conceive of any life apart from their families. Relatives embraced each other with streaming eyes and unabashed displays of emotion.

The departing men were ordered to draw up into columns six deep and to line up to the left of the other Acadian men.

Colonel Winslow put all of his soldiers under arms. Eighty soldiers under the command of Captain Adams were given charge of the men preparing to leave, but even when faced with the fixed bayonets of Adams' men, the young Acadians refused to move when the order was given to march. Their pleas and curses fell on deaf ears, and when Adams' soldiers advanced with fixed bayonets to enforce the command, the men, prodded with cold steel, were finally compelled to move.

As the gates of the enclosure swung open, the women of Grand Pré, alerted by the commotion that something was afoot, rushed from their homes and lined the road to the river landing. Women called out to their husbands and sons as they passed in the mournful procession and followed them, weeping and wringing their hands. Theresa Landry, who was just five feet tall, stood on tiptoe, twisting and turning to peer around the English redcoats who marched on either side of the departing men, straining for a glimpse of Philippe Bernard.

"Philippe!" she shouted when she spotted him. "You must get word to me which ship you're on!"

When Philippe spotted Theresa, his crestfallen expression changed to one of joy. "I will! I will! I'll get word to you somehow!"

When her sons and stepsons passed by, Marie-Jeanne Landry broke into her favorite hymn. "Everything changes, under the heavens," she sang in a deep contralto. It was a mournful hymn about the transitory nature of all human striving, and of life itself. The hymn was quickly picked up by the other women, and finally by the marching men themselves:

> *"Tout passe—*
> *Sous le firmament—*
> *Tout n'est que changement—*
> *Tout passe—*
> *C'est le mérite*
> *Hormis l'éternité*
> *Tout passe—*
> *Paisons valoir la grâce*
> *Le temps est précieux*
> *Ouvrez devant nos yeux*
> *Tout passe—"*

At the river landing, the young men were loaded into boats and rowed out to the five ships in the harbor. The village women crowded the riverbank, straining for a last glimpse. Finally, they turned for home, silent and dejected, too downcast to speak.

Chapter Five

The night after Philippe and the other men were loaded onto the ships in the harbor, Theresa and her family were startled by a loud knock. For once, Theresa was the first to struggle out of sleep, light a candle, and stumble to the door. Her mother, her heart beating wildly with the hope that her husband had been released, was not far behind. Theresa could hardly believe her eyes when she saw Philippe Bernard standing on the threshold of her home, dripping wet. In a moment, he was inside, blowing out her candle and cautioning them all to silence.

"Some of us overpowered the guards on board the *Dolphin* and swam ashore," he said in a whisper, his hand raking through his hair. "The redcoats will be hot on my trail." No sooner had he spoken than the Landrys heard shouts mingled with the sound of galloping horses. Philippe slipped into the Landrys' armoire and hid himself behind the women's clothing hanging inside, only a moment before two soldiers entered.

"Have you seen a young man in wet clothes?" one of them asked.

"Why, no, we haven't seen a thing," said Theresa, grateful that her father had taught her some English.

"What are you doing up at this hour?" the other one asked suspiciously.

"We heard noise and came to see what it was," she said with her sweetest smile. The soldier looked at the diminutive but full-bodied girl, her mass of black curls spilling down her back, and was taken in by the innocent look in her huge dark eyes. The other one was not so gullible.

"We'd better have a look," he said, pushing past her into the house. While he searched her room, the other soldier ran upstairs to the boys' sleeping loft, empty now that Claude and René were gone. They both converged on the main room, shaking their heads. One of the soldiers cast a suspicious eye at the armoire, and Theresa thought that she would faint when he opened it and began jabbing at her clothes with his bayonet.

"Nothing here," he said. "We'd better move on before he escapes us entirely. Let us know if you see anyone," he said to Theresa.

"Yes, I will," she said sweetly.

As soon as the soldiers had gone, she flew to the armoire, only to see a laughing Philippe emerge from a tangle of feminine garments, uninjured. "Someone must be watching over me. One of those jabs missed me by this much," he said, holding his fingers an inch apart. He turned toward Theresa.

"We've got to leave now. We've not a moment to lose."

"Where are you taking my daughter?" Madame Landry interjected.

"We'll hide in the woods until I can find Left Foot," he said, naming a Micmac Indian who occasionally traded with the Acadians. "He'll take care of us until the English stop looking for me. Then we can go to Quebec."

"Quebec?" Madame Landry asked dully. Events were moving too fast for her. Theresa had already thrown on her clothes and returned. Marie-Jeanne knew that her husband had forbidden Theresa to see Philippe, but she herself was not immune to the young man's charm and thought that it made more sense for Theresa to run away with the man she loved than to sit around waiting to be deported. If only her husband were there to consult! "You can't leave without your father's permission."

"Please don't talk to me of permission. I must stay with Philippe any way I can, Mama. I'm going!"

"What shall I tell Gaspard?"

"Tell him you forbade me but I ran away. He won't blame you," Theresa replied.

"At least put on some dry clothes," Madame Landry said to Philippe, accepting the inevitable. While he dressed in a dry shirt and a pair of Claude's trousers, she made them a package of bread and meat, which Theresa wrapped in a blanket from her bed.

"Lend me Claude's gun," Philippe said when he was dressed. "I've got gold—my sister smuggled it into the church with my food—so we should be able to establish ourselves in Quebec," he said in response to Madame Landry's anxious looks. "It's better than being herded like cattle against our will."

After a hasty kiss for her mother, Theresa joined Philippe on the porch. The redcoats had concluded their search in Theresa's neighborhood, and the street was empty. It was a clear, bright night, with a full moon and a thousand brilliant stars. Theresa and Philippe slipped stealthily from house to house.

"We'll have to head for cover," said Philippe. "My luck could have extended to a dark night." He glanced around before continuing. "The soldiers have all gone, but they'll be back."

"Where shall we go, Philippe?" Theresa asked.

He pointed over a bare wheat field to a clump of willow trees in the distance. "It will take us half an hour to get there, and we'll have little cover on the way, but we'll have to risk it. Hang on." He took her by the hand and began running as fast as he could, dragging Theresa, with her short legs, behind him. She ran until she thought she would burst from the pain in her side.

"We're almost there," said Philippe when he heard Theresa's breath coming in rapid gasps. No sooner had they reached the clump of trees than they heard voices ahead. A small group of soldiers were conferring. Theresa and Philippe took refuge behind a large willow tree and waited.

"Can you understand what they are saying?" Philippe whispered.

"The one who seems to be the leader says there's no one here and told the others to look farther, in the forest."

"Good. Our best bet is to stay here for the night. We were lucky to miss them in the clearing. They'll check deeper in the woods and keep an eye on the open space we just crossed from the town, but I doubt that they'll be back here. Fortune is on our side," he said, smiling down at her with the look that always melted her heart. Then he stooped and gave her a long kiss that sent a deep shudder through her whole frame.

Theresa dropped her bundle to the ground and threw her arms around Philippe. They sank slowly onto her blanket, devouring each other with kisses. The wind soughed gently through the long fronds of the willow trees, swaying them gently to and fro, and a thousand stars looked down upon them.

"Remember, love, if they should capture me again, I'm on board a ship called the *Dolphin*," Philippe whispered as he unbuttoned her dress.

"I'll remember," she said. "The *Dolphin*." They looked into each other's eyes as though they wished to memorize the act of love, to crystallize it and carry it with them forever. The thought lay between them, unspoken: this could be the last time. Afterward they lay in each other's arms, spent, and fell into a deep sleep of exhaustion and contentment. The last thing Theresa thought as she drifted off to sleep was: whatever they do to us, whatever may follow, I will have this to remember.

The next morning, Philippe shook Theresa's shoulder gently in the the misty gray shortly before dawn. Theresa sat up, blinking and confused, before the events of the night came back to her. "We've got to leave now, before full light," Philippe said. He pulled her to her feet, and the two of them began walking, Theresa's short legs pumping to keep up with Philippe's smooth, rapid stride. She was hungry, but it was impossible to unwrap the food from her blanket and keep moving at the same time. "We've got to get a horse," she panted after a few minutes. "I can't keep up with you."

Philippe raised his hand, cautioning her to silence. They

were moving south, toward the protection of the forest, which they reached by the time daylight had removed their cover. Philippe was walking so fast that Theresa had to clench her teeth to keep from moaning from the pain in her side. She pressed doggedly on and found that by concentrating on the ground she was able to block out some of the pain. After walking for what seemed like hours, just as she was about to protest that she could go no farther, Philippe stopped in a thicket of pines and gave the same whistle he used to summon her—the long, low call of the whippoorwill. Theresa was too tired to speak and stood gasping for breath as Philippe repeated the call.

Out of the forest stepped a tall, lean Indian dressed in soft deerskin. Despite his rapid stride, Theresa could see that he limped. "Left Foot?" she whispered, regaining her breath at last.

"Yes," Philippe replied. He had told Theresa that Left Foot limped as the result of an old hunting accident.

Philippe and the Micmac raised their hands in greeting. Left Foot took in the situation at a glance. "You need a horse," he said, never questioning how Philippe had escaped from the redcoats, "but first cover flaming hair."

He led them to a small huddle of tepees, where a flat-faced Indian woman gazed impassively at Theresa. Left Foot lifted the flap of one of the tepees and led Philippe and Theresa inside. There he gave Philippe a pot of bear grease, which Philippe began mixing in his hair, while Left Foot pasted a dark red substance on his skin that seemed to change Philippe's face into that of an Indian. Deerskin shirt and pants and soft leather moccasins completed the transformation. As the two worked, Left Foot stole several glances at Theresa, who had removed the food her mother had given them and was eating it. She knew he was thinking Philippe would have a much better chance of escaping without her, but he would never question Philippe's decision to take her with him.

"Squaw's face needs paint, too," was all he said, "and she must be wrapped in Indian blanket." Philippe painted her face while she pulled her hair back and plaited it into a long braid at his command. Left Foot fetched a blanket and showed her how to wrap herself as an Indian female would do.

"Now for the horse," Left Foot said.

"No horse yet," Philippe replied. "We're going to Quebec."

"Quebec?" For an instant, Theresa actually saw surprise written on the Indian's stoic features. "That means crossing great water," he said, motioning toward the bay, "or going far around and over the Cobequid Mountains."

"If you could get us over the water, we could buy a horse on the other side," Philippe said. "I have gold."

"Too risky with squaw," Left Foot replied. "Redcoats are everywhere. They would question our reason for crossing the water. Without the squaw, yes. With her, no." He was not reproaching Philippe for being so foolhardy as to bring a woman along, simply explaining his appraisal of the situation.

"It will take much longer if we go over the mountains," Theresa said. She knew that Quebec was far to the northwest. How to get there, she had no idea, as she had never been outside of Grand Pré before, but she knew it was a long, dangerous journey.

"But safer. And I can give you a good horse." With that, Left Foot disappeared, but he returned five minutes later with a beautiful piebald stallion. "No better horse anywhere," he said.

Philippe unbuttoned his shirt and reached for the money belt he wore next to his skin.

"No money," said Left Foot. "For friendship."

"Let me pay you," said Philippe. "It's far too valuable."

"No money," said Left Foot. The two men looked steadily into each other's eyes, sad with the knowledge that they would probably never see each other again.

"Thank you," said Philippe. "For everything, for all the times you helped me."

"No thanks between friends," said the Indian.

Philippe mounted the horse and helped Theresa up behind him. Left Foot stepped forward with small pots of bear grease and face paint and a pouch of dried beef jerky. "Bread go stale," he said. "Beef jerky last forever."

With a click of his tongue and gentle pressure on the reins of his new horse, Philippe and Theresa were off. For the first few miles, she luxuriated in the comfort of being carried by the horse and adjusted to the rhythm of its body beneath hers.

She put her arms around Philippe's narrow waist and hugged him, staring with fascination at the soft patch of hair, growing to a point, that nestled between the two bones at the nape of his neck. She marveled, once again, at every part of his well-knit body—his beautifully molded head and the proud, erect way it sat on his lean but strong shoulders and the first few vertebrae of his back, which showed above his deerskin jacket. On an impulse, she leaned forward and kissed the nape of his neck. He shuddered involuntarily, and gooseflesh rose where her lips had touched him.

"Enough of that until tonight," he said with a laugh. "I've got to keep my mind on keeping us alive." She could tell that they were skirting Grand Pré, swinging around it in a wide circle to the northeast.

She sighed with contentment and leaned forward, letting her head rest on his back. She was safe with Philippe; she knew the two of them would escape. Philippe could do anything.

For two days and nights, they traveled, veering back to the west once they were clear of Grand Pré. At night, they washed in a cool stream and curled up to sleep beneath their blankets, Theresa as content as a child on holiday. They made love ravenously, making use of their first days of total access to each other's bodies like a pair of gluttons at a banquet. Afterward, they fell asleep blissfully in each other's arms, hardly able to believe that at last they did not have to worry about escaping detection. Each morning, they repainted each other's faces, laughing at the way they looked.

"When we reach Quebec, I'll buy you a ring, and we'll be married by a priest," Philippe promised.

Whenever they spotted redcoats, they hid behind the nearest cover. Once they were surprised, running into a small knot of them unexpectedly. There was nothing for it but to ride by. Theresa's heart was thudding so loudly she was sure they could hear it. She lowered her eyes and tried her best to look like a passive obedient Indian woman. The soldiers only glanced at them. "Just an Injun and his squaw," one of them said.

Early on their third morning together, they were awakened

by shouts. Two soldiers kicked Philippe in the side, their bayonets pointed at his breast. Another redcoat stood hard by.

Philippe and Theresa gazed into each other's eyes, exchanging a long, slow look. There was no need for words. Philippe shrugged as he was dragged roughly to his feet. A soldier tied his hands behind him. "We gave them a run for their money, didn't we?" he said with a grin. "Don't worry, love. If your father couldn't keep us apart, I won't let a little thing like the English army stand in our way. Remember, the *Dolphin*." Theresa was dragged roughly to her feet and bound, too, and then the two of them were put back on their horse. Hands and feet bound so that they could not even touch each other, they were led back to captivity, the reins of their horse tied to the saddle of one of the English soldier's. There had apparently been a bounty out for the capture of the "Red Fox," because there was great jesting among the soldiers as to what they would do with the money. They took pleasure in taunting Philippe, jabbing the butts of their muskets in his face and hurling insults at him that made Theresa's ears burn. They refused to give either one anything to eat or drink.

The trip back only took one day of hard riding, but Theresa found defeat more fatiguing than any amount of strenuous physical effort. She did not know if they had ever had a real chance, but it seemed to her that they had come so close to escaping . . . but she put such thoughts out of her mind. Now she must bend all of her efforts toward keeping the two of them together, even if they were in captivity.

They reached Grand Pré long after nightfall, but the soldiers went at once to the priest's home where Colonel Winslow was headquartered, leaving Philippe and Theresa, still bound, outside the palisade on their mount. Winslow came running out at once, still buttoning his scarlet coat over his capacious belly. At the sight of Philippe, his face broke into a cruel smile. "So the 'Red Fox' has had his tail clipped, eh? I'll show you how we treat rebels." At his command, two of the soldiers lit torches.

Winslow and the three soldiers mounted their horses, and led Philippe and Theresa slowly through the town. Theresa was glad that the citizens of Grand Pré were abed and not out to witness their humiliation. Before Philippe's house, Colonel

Winslow bade the soldiers stop. He gave an abrupt order to one of the soldiers to remove the inhabitants of the house.

"What are they saying? What are they going to do?" Philippe asked.

"Your family is to be removed. I don't know why," Theresa replied. Frightened screams came from inside Philippe's home, and in a few minutes his widowed mother and those brothers and sisters who still remained at home were herded out into the night in their night clothes.

"Philippe!" his mother shouted when she saw him. "Oh, my boy!" She held out her arms to him, but a soldier pushed her roughly back.

"Torch the house," Colonel Winslow commanded.

Before his mother's horrified eyes, the two soldiers ran about the house, setting the dry wood and thatched roof on fire. The house was a roaring blaze in minutes.

Philippe tried to turn his eyes aside, but Colonel Winslow took his head roughly and turned it toward the flames. "Be glad we didn't put you on a spit and roast you like the insubordinate pig that you are," he rasped.

Madame Bernard, a long gray braid hanging down beneath her nightcap, put her face in her hands and wept as her home went up in flames. Then, as Philippe watched anxiously, she doubled over, clutching her heart.

"She's got a bad heart. This could kill her," Philippe said. He turned toward Winslow. "If my mother dies, I'll kill you," he said quietly. Winslow drew back his hand and struck Philippe in the face just as the beams of his home collapsed with a great crashing sound, sending a shower of flames and sparks into the night.

When the blaze had subsided to a pile of smoldering embers, Winslow turned toward his men. "Put Bernard back on the ships and send his little whore home. As for them," he said with a sweep of his hand toward Philippe's mother and family, "let someone take them in." By that time, half of Grand Pré had turned out to watch the sad spectacle, and there were any number of volunteers to offer shelter to Philippe's family.

"Take my mother home with you, Theresa," Philippe shouted as he was dragged off.

"I will," Theresa called after him, "and I'll get on the *Dolphin* somehow."

Unbound at last, Theresa took the old woman, who was still clutching her heart and breathing in a most peculiar way, by the hand and led her home. Her own family had been alerted to what had happened, and there was no need to explain. Theresa's mother put Madame Bernard to bed in the great bed by the fire and sent her two young boys with Theresa and Claire. Theresa, exhausted, fell asleep at once. When she rose the next morning, she was informed that Madame Bernard had died of heart failure during the night.

Chapter Six

Slowly, ominously, the bay began filling with ships. By the first week of October, there were fourteen vessels in the harbor, and Colonel Winslow decided that he could wait no longer. On the morning he sent out the command for departure, Marie-Jeanne Landry bade one last tearful farewell to her home, tucked her children on top of the hay wagon that was laden with her household goods, and stepped up into the driver's seat. She flapped the reins, and her husband's best team of oxen joined the stream of traffic moving slowly to the landing on the Gaspereau River. Before they arrived, she reminded her daughters to stay out of sight as much as possible. There were British guards everywhere.

Theresa, sitting beside her mother with her brother Richard in her lap, surveyed the scene with horror. Never had she witnessed such woe and confusion. Ursule Hebert was lifting her frail grandmother onto a makeshift bed in their wagon, as the old lady was too weak to walk. Theresa's friend, Anne Bonin, pregnant with her third child, walked beside her wagon, afraid of the jolting ride.

At the landing, the older Acadian men were allowed to join their families. The English redcoats in charge of loading the boats managed to convey to the women that there was no room on the ships for anything but members of their family and that all of their possessions must be left behind. A loud wail rose from the women, who had spent days deciding which of their belongings were absolutely essential and which could be left behind. The soldiers, most of whom did not speak a word of French, ignored the women's protests and lifted them, half struggling, into the boats, which rocked gently in the water.

Theresa, her parents, her younger sister, Claire, and her brothers, Evariste and Richard, were shoved into a boat and began moving downriver toward the bay. Theresa strained her eyes, trying to decipher the names on the ships, while her mother looked back in tears as her armoire receded in the distance.

Their boat drew abreast of the first of the English ships, which rocked in its moorings, its great sails bellying in the wind. "Please, sir, we go on the *Dolphin*?" she said hopefully to one of their escorts.

"No, miss, that ship's full."

"Which one is the *Dolphin*?"

"That one, there," he said, pointing to the ship they were approaching. Theresa's heart began thudding wildly as they drew abreast of the ship. She turned to her sister and little brothers with a look of tender love in her eye. "Good-bye, Claire, and be happy." Before Claire could respond, Theresa stood up and walked to where her parents were seated. "I must get to Philippe. You'll always be with me," she said with tears flowing down her cheeks. Theresa turned and ran for the guard rail. She took a deep breath and threw herself over the side of the boat. She surfaced, gasping for air and spitting out salt water. Ignoring her mother's screams, she tried to crawl through the water but felt herself being pulled under by her clothing. She had several yards to go to grasp the rough hemp rope ladder still dangling over the side of the vessel. She went under a second time and stayed under until she thought her lungs would burst, but she flailed underwater until the ladder was almost within reach. Theresa's body went limp, and she realized she would not make it.

Just as she felt her lungs exploding, a strong arm grasped her hair and pulled her to the surface. A sailor from the

Dolphin came to her rescue and pulled her up the ladder until she was within the grasp of the men leaning over the side of the vessel. Two men on board seized her beneath the arms and pulled her over the side of the ship. She lay in a sodden heap, panting and exhausted, and looked from face to face, searching the crowd for Philippe. He was not there.

Her cousin, Leon, bent over her, his face filled with concern. "Why would you do a thing like that, Theresa? You almost drowned."

"Philippe," she whispered as soon as she could speak. "I had to be with Philippe. Where is he?"

"He's not here anymore. The group who escaped were broken up and put on different ships."

"I don't believe it! It can't be true!"

"I'm sorry, but it is," Leon replied stiffly.

Theresa lay against her cousin's shoulder, a small, wet lump of misery. Not only had she lost Philippe, but she had lost her family, as well. She was alone, heading for an unknown destination with nothing but the clothes on her back and Leon for a companion. She gazed up at her cousin. Leon was a strong, sturdy young man with a powerful build. He was considered to be an excellent match by the young girls of Grand Pré, but somehow Theresa could never bring herself to enjoy his company. Now she was forced to.

As soon as she could, Theresa walked over to the ship's rail and gazed out over the bay. She heard a low moan, growing into a loud wail, which spread quickly from ship to ship.

Theresa looked up. In the distance, she could see flames leaping into the sky. "What is happening, Leon?" she asked her cousin, who was standing by her side.

"They're burning Grand Pré," he answered in a harsh voice, his hand tightening on her elbow until she almost cried out from the pain. "They're burning our homes. Damn the English!"

Theresa hung her head and began crying. "Don't cry, Theresa," said Leon, putting his arm around her in a proprietary manner. "I'll take care of you."

*   *   *

Three days out of Grand Pré, Philippe Bernard led a mutiny on the *Pembroke*, the ship he had been placed on after his aborted escape attempt. The ship was taken over by the Acadians on board and steered back to the mouth of the Minas Bay. Not knowing what else to do, most of those on board the *Pembroke* returned to the smoking ruins of their homes. When Acadia was resettled by the British, the Acadians still in the area were hired to repair the dikes, with the result that they became servants on the property they had formerly owned.

Philippe Bernard, alone among the Acadians on board the *Pembroke*, returned to Grand Pré only to fulfill a promise. Easily overpowering the guards outside the stockade around the Church of St. Charles, who had relaxed their vigilance now that the Acadians were deported, he strode boldly through the front door of the priest's home and entered Col. John Winslow's bedroom. Winslow, dressed in a long nightshirt and wearing a warm nightcap against the autumn chill, was awakened from a sound sleep by the blade of a steel knife that tickled the fold between his two chins. He lived long enough to see that his assailant was Philippe Bernard and to whine for pity in a terrified voice before Philippe stuck the knife into his throat and slit it neatly from ear to ear. As Colonel Winslow's lifeblood gushed and bubbled out over his fine linen nightshirt, Philippe said, "That is for killing my mother."

With that, he wiped his knife on Winslow's bedsheets, slipped out into the night, and turned resolutely toward the south.

Now, he said to himself, I am going to find Theresa.

Chapter Seven

On a crisp November day the Dolphin *sailed up the Choptank* River in the English colony of Maryland, dropped anchor at the little town of Oxford, and disgorged its stunned human cargo onto a wharf lined with hogsheads of tobacco. Theresa, dizzy and weak from hunger and inactivity, clung to her Cousin Leon's arm as they descended the gangplank. The bright light made her eyes water, and she shielded her face against the rays of the morning sun. The wretched victims of the dispersion were herded into an empty warehouse in which a small group of local citizens had congregated to look over the new arrivals for possible servants. Theresa hung her head and submitted to the indignity of being scrutinized, her feelings too dulled by the ordeal of her journey to care that she was being examined like a side of beef. Again and again, scenes from the *Dolphin*'s voyage passed through her mind.

Until the ranks of the Acadians were thinned by death, the ship had been so crowded that forty people had been forced to sleep on the open deck. Every Acadian, none of whom had ever been on a vessel larger than a fishing boat, suffered the nausea and vomiting of seasickness. Theresa retched until her sides ached and refused at first to eat and drink the dirty water, aged salt pork, and wormy biscuits that were their only sustenance.

To add to their woes, a dreadful storm arose on the second day out, tossing the ship, until only her desire to be reunited with Philippe kept Theresa from praying for death. Several of those who slept on the deck were swept overboard, and the *Dolphin* was so buffeted by waves that most of her passengers despaired of reaching land. The Acadians were driven at last to eat the ship's miserable fare, which began to have its effects almost at once, producing dysentery, headaches, boils, scurvy, and constipation. Theresa prayed for a fresh drop of water or a good piece of bread as she lay listlessly in the hold, dreaming of her mother's hearty meals.

A few days after the storm subsided, smallpox and ship fever broke out. A mild attack of smallpox suffered when she was a child had given Theresa a natural immunity to the disease, and ship fever also passed her by, but many friends and neighbors were not so fortunate. The very old and very young were the first to die. Ursule Hebert's grandmother died a week into the journey, and the infant son of Clarisse and Alexandre Bergeron died the following day. Clarisse Bergeron was only two years older than Theresa, and the two girls had long been friends. Theresa was deeply concerned when Clarisse refused to relinquish her baby's corpse. She lay huddled in a corner, rocking the limp body and crooning, refusing to take any kind of nourishment. When Theresa tried to coax her into eating, Clarisse sat staring at her with dull eyes, as if she had never seen her friend before, but she finally allowed her jaws to be pried open and acepted a few bits of bread and pork.

"Chew," Theresa commanded her. Clarisse obediently moved her jaws up and down, obeying like a small child.

"Don't you think it's time to give up Michel?" Theresa asked gently when she saw that she was getting some response. Clarisse emitted a sound that was a cross between a whine and a snarl and clutched the dead infant to her bosom.

When the corpse began to smell, Alexandre had to wrest it from his wife's arms, prying her fingers from it one by one, and with a few prayers the unfortunate child was tossed into its watery grave. After Michel was buried at sea, Clarisse sat with her knees drawn up to her chest, staring blankly with glazed eyes. She refused to respond to those around her. Two weeks into the voyage, she contracted smallpox and died without putting up a struggle.

The only other infant on board the *Dolphin* was the son of Adolphe and Marguerite Guidry. Marguerite lost her milk, from either the miserable diet or the trauma of being ejected from her home, and was forced to watch helplessly as her baby slowly starved to death. Standing in the warehouse, Theresa shuddered as she remembered the baby's wails of hunger. For days after the child died, Theresa had been unable to forget his cries. They had even haunted her dreams.

During the voyage, Theresa came to rely more and more heavily on Leon, who provided her with a sturdy shoulder to sleep against and tried to take her mind off her misery by reminding her of happier days in Grand Pré. The deportees understood at last that they were being scattered among the thirteen English colonies, and Theresa and Leon exchanged vows to find their families.

Theresa slowly began to develop some affection for her quiet cousin. She and her sister Claire used to laugh at the way Leon talked—slowly and deliberately, with a touch of pomposity, as though he thought his words ought to be recorded for posterity. He was one of the few men in the Landry family who shared her father's love of books, and this had always made him appear a bit formidable, but the enforced intimacy of life on board the ship helped Theresa break through his wall of reserve. He was not a bad fellow if one could forgive the excessively high opinion he had of himself; and she even reached the conclusion that with his dark brown eyes and wavy black hair, he would not be a bad-looking man if his face ever stopped breaking out. But when, after almost a month at sea, he asked her to marry him, she declined his offer as gently as she could. She would marry no one but Philippe Bernard.

Leon, for his part, was delighted that he and Theresa had been thrown together by circumstance. He had adored his pretty cousin for years and could not understand why he was so shy in her presence when he was liked well enough by everyone else in Grand Pré. The profound suspicion most Acadians felt toward anyone with intellectual inclinations had been overcome to some extent in Leon's case by his sense of responsibility and his capacity for hard work. Although he was only seventeen, he had been one of the first men called upon when a barn burned or a newly married couple needed a house built. He knew there were many young girls in Grand Pré who would jump at the chance to marry him, but he had no interest in anyone but his cousin.

After numerous attempts to approach Theresa the summer before deportation, during which his nerve always failed him at the last moment, Leon had decided that he would wait until she was a year older to begin wooing her. He was determined to make her his wife. Night after night, he lay in the sleeping loft of his home, dreaming of her, aching for her. Nor was his attraction to her merely physical. Leon had thought about it carefully and decided she would make an ideal wife. Her pedigree was above reproach—almost identical, in fact, to his own—and she had been well trained by her mother. Her vivacity and gaiety would offset his natural reserve, and he thought that her exposure to her father's literary side would prevent her from resenting his own. After they were married, she would grow to be proud of his erudition. He did not, of course, expect her to share his interest in books. A literary woman, to Leon, was a total abomination, if, indeed, he could imagine living with such a creature. Women existed to make life warm and comfortable and pleasant, to bear one's children and run one's household, and to gaze upon men like Leon with adoring eyes.

His plans for the two of them had been shaken by the appearance of Philippe Bernard. Leon had watched with horror Theresa's interest in Philippe grow month by month. What could Theresa see in him? he had asked himself. It was true that Philippe was a handsome man who made small talk effortlessly. He could flirt and tease with an abandon Leon would never possess, and the village girls were always laughing at something he had said. Leon had examined some of Philippe's remarks carefully, and he did not find them to be particularly amusing or clever. Besides, Leon could not understand why women set so much store by such frivolous qualities. Of what use were they in the long run? What did they count for when a man and woman settled down to the serious business of building a home and raising a family? Surely Theresa would mature and realize that she would be a fool to throw herself away on Philippe when she could have him instead, Leon reasoned. He was limp with relief when he heard that Gaspard Landry had forbidden the match, but Gaspard's refusal did not remove his anxiety over his standing with Theresa. There would be other contenders for her hand; he should make his move soon.

In September, Leon managed to convey to Gaspard that when he considered the time to be ripe, he would ask for Theresa's hand. Leon's father, Charles Landry, was Gaspard's first cousin, and the two men had grown up practically as brothers. Nothing would have pleased Gaspard more than a match between the two. With Gaspard on his side, Leon had been convinced that Theresa would accept him in time.

When Theresa had been hauled aboard the *Dolphin*, almost drowned and choking up salt water, Leon's heart had begun thudding so violently that he thought it would surely leap out of his chest. For days he had sat in abject misery, his mind filled with gloomy thoughts of the loss of his home, his family, and Theresa. He had no illusions about the intentions of the English. He knew that the Acadians were being stripped of all they owned and thrown onto foreign soil where they would be treated with hostility because they were French. The thought of servitude to strangers galled him unbearably. That he, the best of the Landrys, should be put in such a position! But he possessed patience, and he would work his way out of the mess somehow.

To the loss of his family and his exalted position in the community was added the equally painful loss of Theresa. Then, miraculously, she had literally been tossed into his lap. True, she had boarded the *Dolphin* in search of Philippe Bernard, but Philippe had been put on another ship after his foolish attempt to escape. She would forget Philippe soon enough. Now, at last, he had the opportunity for which he had waited. She would get to know him slowly; she would learn to appreciate him. If he could win Theresa, all would not be lost.

Throughout the ordeal of their voyage, he stuck resolutely by her side, giving her his food if it seemed less miserable than hers, shielding her from wind and cold as best he could. She rested on his arm at night, and there were times when his arm went numb from her weight, but he would not move her to relieve the pressure for fear of waking her.

When he asked her to marry him at last, he was only slightly discouraged by her refusal. He was, if anything, angry at himself for having moved too soon. The prospect of the end of their voyage and the fear that they would be separated when they arrived at their destination made him act hastily. He would simply have to contrive to keep in close touch with her after they landed. Surely she would rely on him more heavily when they were both strangers in a foreign land. Maryland, Captain Griffiths had told them the day before they dropped anchor at Oxford. They were being taken to the colony of Maryland.

In the tobacco warehouse where the Acadians had been herded out of the raw November wind, Leon was approached almost at once by a poorly clad man with shifty eyes. He pried Leon's jaw opened and examined his teeth carefully.

"Tell him to show me his muscles," he said to Captain Griffiths.

"He understands you," the captain replied. "That one speaks some English."

Leon obediently rolled up his sleeves and tensed his biceps. The shifty-eyed man squeezed the bulging muscles and whistled softly.

"I'll take this one," he said. "What's your name, boy?"

Leon surveyed the man before him with distaste but knew that he must appear to be servile and respectful to survive.

"Leon Landry, sir."

"You go with him," said Captain Griffiths, glad to be relieved so easily of one of his charges.

"Please, where are you taking me?" Leon asked.

"My name's Caleb Wheeler—Mr. Wheeler to you—and I'm the overseer on the Ramsey plantation acrost the river," he said, jerking his head toward the water.

"Can we take my cousin, too?" Leon pleaded.

Caleb Wheeler looked Theresa over slowly from head to toe with a stare that made her turn hot with shame. He spat a

51

long stream of tobacco juice onto the floor of the warehouse. "Cousin, eh?" he said with a smirking grin that exposed rotten teeth. "I don't blame you for wanting to take her with you, but we've plenty of female slaves to do the women's work."

"At least let me stay with her until she's claimed. I'm the only family she's got."

"All right, if it don't take too long. I've got a little business to take care of. When I git back, we're leaving, ready or not."

As Wheeler sauntered off, Theresa became aware that she was being examined by an older man. He had a thick mane of gray hair, a red face marked by small broken blood vessels, and small eyes that seemed swallowed up in a face too large for them. He was overweight, but the superb cut of his fawn coat helped to disguise his thickening middle. His linen was clean and starched, and lace showed beneath his sleeves and spilled down his coat front. His boots were worn but made of expensive leather. Once again, Theresa flushed hotly at the way his eyes raked over her. He looked her up one side and down the other as if she were a piece of furniture he was considering purchasing. He, in turn, found himself gazing at a voluptuous young girl whose pale, delicate face was dominated by a pair of huge eyes as deep and lustrous as black velvet. Her face was framed prettily by a mass of curly black hair. When the man caught Theresa's eye, he approached Captain Griffiths.

"I'm looking for a white female to run my dispensary. I need someone who's intelligent and industrious. What do you know about that girl?"

"All these Frenchies are alike to me," said Griffiths with a shrug. He started to add that he would not trust any one of them, but he realized that he had a whole shipload of them to dispose of and restrained himself. "I think she speaks a little English—none of the other women do. You'll have to examine her yourself."

The man turned to face Theresa. "My name is Dr. Edmund McIntyre. What is your name?" he said, speaking slowly and distinctly.

"Theresa Landry."

52

"You speak English?"

"Yes," she said. *"Un peu*—I mean, a little."

"How old are you?"

Theresa searched her mind, trying to remember the English word for "sixteen." Her father had taught her a little English, more as a game than anything else, never dreaming that she would be called on to use it. When she was a child, she would point to objects, and Gaspard would tell her the English words for them. She had learned to put simple sentences together, but she could only count to ten.

"I have so many years," she said, holding up all ten fingers. She closed her hands and then opened them and held up six fingers.

"Do you know anything about medicine?"

She turned to Leon, bewildered.

"Le médicament, le remède," he translated.

"A little," she replied. Like all Acadian housewives, Theresa's mother had had a herb bed from which she made simple home remedies, and she had passed what she knew on to her daughters. Leon explained this to the doctor.

"She'll do," said Dr. McIntyre to Captain Griffiths.

Theresa turned to her cousin. "He's all right," he said to her in French. "And you'll learn something useful from him. He wants you to run a place that dispenses medicine.

"Please, sir, where do you live?" Leon asked the doctor in English.

"In a red brick house on the town square. Anyone can direct you to it."

Leon was relieved that Theresa was not being taken off into the country somewhere. "You go with him," he said to her. "I'll come to see you when ever I can."

"Please, Leon, I don't want to go with this man. I don't trust him." She spoke rapidly in French, hoping the doctor could not understand.

"You have little choice. What is it about him that you dislike?"

"The way he looks at me makes me feel uncomfortable."

"You're a pretty girl. You'll find that most strange men look at you that way."

"Very well," she said, sighing. She would trust Leon's

53

judgment, and it appeared that she had no choice in the matter. "Thank you for being so good to me, Leon."

"I'll always love you. Don't forget that." Leon put his arms around her and gave her a prim kiss on the forehead. Just as he released her, Caleb Wheeler appeared in the doorway, laden with two heavy sacks.

"Take these, boy. Look lively, now." With one last look of longing, Leon shouldered Wheeler's burdens and set off.

Theresa followed her new master out into the sunlight, where he helped her into a mud-spattered barouche drawn by a pair of matched gray horses. Dr. McIntyre took the reins, and with a flick of his whip they were off, clattering down the cobblestones of the street leading to Oxford's main square. They drew up before a house of red brick that made Theresa draw in her breath. It was the finest home she had ever seen. As Dr. McIntyre helped her out of the barouche and steered her up the marble steps to her new home, she was uncomfortably aware that he was squeezing her arm, and he walked much closer to her than was necessary.

Chapter Eight

The door to the McIntyre house was opened by a dignified black man. "Good morning, Moses," said Dr. McIntyre, handing him his cloak.

"Good morning, sir," said Moses with a slight bow. His eyes rested briefly on Theresa, but the expression on his face did not change, and he did not address her. Theresa, who had never seen a black person before, tried not to gape in astonishment at the man or at the rooms of the house, which had a spaciousness, airiness, and elegance she had never even imagined. Nor had she ever seen so clean a place. Although her mother had been a tidy housekeeper, Theresa was to learn that her new mistress had an obsession with cleanliness that bordered on mania.

A premonitory chill ran down Theresa's spine at the heavy silence. Despite the luxurious surroundings, she knew that she had not entered a happy place. Why, exactly, she could not say, but the very air seemed laden with tension. Her own home had been a happy one, full of the inevitable minor eruptions that occur when people live together but free from major disturbances, and she knew immediately that the household of which she was now a part was not of that kind.

Dr. McIntyre directed Theresa to a sitting room where his

wife sat with a basket of sewing. Theresa thought at once that they were an odd match. She had had time to study the doctor on their trip to his home after he stopped ogling her. The doctor carried with him a definite air of authority and hearty exuberance. He exuded a healthy masculine scent of leather, horses, and tobacco that brought tears to Theresa's eyes as she remembered her father. Mrs. McIntyre, on the other hand, was a dry, thin woman, about the same age as her husband, with a narrow, pinched face and gray hair drawn back severely at the nape of her neck. She was wearing a plain dress of black wool whose only ornaments were white cuffs and a lace collar on which an onyx and gold mourning brooch had been pinned.

She rose when they entered and looked Theresa over from head to toe. "This is Theresa Landry, Elizabeth," said Dr. McIntyre. "She was on the ship of Frenchmen from Nova Scotia. She'll be working in the dispensary with Pammy."

Mrs. McIntyre's lip curled into a bitter, contemptuous smile. "A felicitous choice, no doubt."

"Now, Elizabeth, you're the one who said that people would rather take medicine from a white woman than from a slave."

"So I did."

"Say hello to your new mistress, Theresa," Dr. McIntyre said to break the awkward silence.

"How do you do?" said Theresa.

"Cheeky wench, isn't she?" said Mrs. McIntyre. "You're to lower your eyes and curtsy when you speak to me, and you must address me as 'ma'am.' "

Theresa looked at Dr. McIntyre, confused. "She only speaks a little English, and I doubt she has been in service before," he explained to his wife.

"You brought her here; you see to it that she learns to behave properly. But I must say, Edmund, that I do not relish the prospect of having a foreigner under my roof, and certainly not a French papist."

"But you will let her stay? She seems to be a bright girl, and servants aren't to be had for the asking. Besides, Elizabeth, we got her free. If she were an indentured servant, we'd have had to pay her passage."

This consideration apparently appeared to Mrs. McIntyre's sense of thrift. "Very well. She may sleep in the attic room, in Betsy's old bed."

Mrs. McIntyre sat down with an air of resignation and picked up her sewing. "The girl's filthy. Tell Puss to burn those rags she's wearing and fit her with new clothes. She's to have a half-tick petticoat, an apron, and two white caps, in addition to two dresses. Of course she'll have to have new shoes and stockings and a shift. Tell Puss to give her a good scrub. And mind you," she said, addressing Theresa directly, "I'll have no curling irons in my house. You're to keep your hair pinned up under your cap." Theresa nodded in assent, although she understood only that she was to be given new clothing and had no idea what a curling iron was. Mrs. McIntyre bent her head over her needle. They had been dismissed.

Dr. McIntyre led Theresa down the central hall of the house and out the back door. Behind the house was a cluster of outbuildings Theresa was later to learn included kitchen and scullery, weaving room and carriage house, the dispensary and a small herb garden, and quarters for the house slaves. On a covered brick breezeway connecting the kitchen to the main house, Theresa saw her second black person. A woman dressed in a colorful calico dress, a red scarf tied around her head, was walking toward the house, bearing a covered platter from which delicious odors emanated. Theresa felt a wave of dizziness at the smell of food and stumbled against her master. Dr. McIntyre took her arm. "You're probably famished," he said. "We'll have Dicey feed you before your bath."

In the kitchen, a fat black woman was bending over an iron stove, putting more food onto another platter. "Good day, Massa Edmund," she said when she spotted the pair. "I just about got your meal on the table."

"It smells delicious, Dicey. This is Theresa. She's to be working with Pammy in the dispensary. I want you to feed her and then send her to Puss to be washed and clothed." He gave Dicey a list of the garments Theresa was to have. Theresa, for her part, almost fainted at the wonderful kitchen smells. She felt a rush of water to her mouth, and a small trickle of saliva escaped and trickled down her chin. She sank weakly onto a bench before a trestle table in the center of the kitchen.

"Whew! She a sight! I won't have no dirty girl in my clean kitchen!" said Dicey, brandishing a large ladle.

"She's come all the way from Nova Scotia on a ship, and as you can see, she's weak from hunger. You feed her first, and then Puss will clean her up." With that, Dr. McIntyre left, leaving Dicey to grumble and shake her head as she heaped a plate with food for Theresa.

"I guess you are hungry," she said as Theresa attacked her plate. "You act like you ain't had a meal in days."

Theresa was too busy eating to answer. She had roast chicken and potatoes, boiled carrots and steaming fluffy biscuits dripping with butter, and some baked dish she did not recognize. She was sure it was the best food she had ever eaten. While she ate, Dicey finished preparing the McIntyres' midday meal, and the black woman Theresa had seen on the breezeway, whom Dicey addressed as Hetty, made two more trips to the house with covered dishes.

"Where dat place Massa say you come from?" Dicey asked as soon as Theresa had finished eating.

"Please, I speak little English," Theresa replied. Try as she might, she could not understand a single word of the soft, slurred black *patois*.

"You one of them Frenchies we fighting now. Lord, I heard they were terrible folk, mean as devils." She studied Theresa carefully. "You look just like plain folks to me, except prettier." She chuckled. "Right away I see why Massa picked you."

Theresa shook her head and shrugged her shoulders. "You come along now. Puss going to wash you and fix you up to look like white folks." Dicey led the way to another building, her ample rump swaying as she made her way slowly across the yard. She led Theresa into a building where a short, muscular black women was folding linen. "This is Theresa. She going to work in the dispensary with Pammy. You got to scrub her and give her some clothes."

Theresa received from Puss the same knowing look she had gotten from the other women. "Massa sho' know how to pick 'em,'' she said. ''She be right pretty once I burn them rags and fix her up. You leave her to me.'' Her nose wrinkled in distaste. ''You, girl, strip down and wrap yourself in this,'' she said, handing her a blanket. Theresa stood staring at her. ''Is you slow?'' Puss demanded.

''She don't know how to talk like a Christian. She French, poor thing,'' said Dicey. ''You got to go slow with her at first, like she was a baby.'' Dicey turned and waddled back to her kitchen as Puss dragged out a large tin tub and conveyed to Theresa through gestures that she was to get in it. While a cauldron of water heated over the fire, Puss fetched shoes and stockings, two linen sleeping shifts, two white linen caps, two handkerchiefs, a petticoat and shirtwaist, and two calico dresses, one brown and one blue.

When the water on the fire was warm, she poured it into the tub and handed Theresa a bar of lye soap. ''Scrub yourself good. Missus don't 'low no dirty girls.'' Theresa sank gratefully into the warm water and closed her eyes, letting the warmth relax the tension in her body. The harsh soap brought tears to her eyes when she washed her hair, but it was good to be clean again. When she was through, Puss helped her dress in the strange new garments and dried her hair before the fire.

Finally, Puss said, ''I take you to see Pammy now,'' and led her to yet another building.

The dispensary was full of strange odors and rows of glass apothecary jars lined up along wooden shelves. Pammy was slim and pretty and younger than the other women. ''This here's Theresa. She's French and don't know how to talk yet. Massa says she's to help run the dispensary.'' Once again, Theresa endured the swift evaluation and the knowing smile.

''You leave her to me.'' After Puss had left, Pammy studied Theresa again and shook her head. ''Massa told me he was sending someone, but I thought at least I'd be able to talk to you. Do you know anything about this?'' she said, waving her hand at the rows of jars. Theresa shrugged her shoulders.

Pammy sighed. ''I guess I got to start at the beginning. You listen to me and say it over and over till you understand. Massa too busy cutting people open and taking care of rich folks to take care of all the people that come to him. I grow the herbs and make the tinctures and decoctions and hand 'em out. You gets the sick folks to tell you what's wrong, and after a while you learn what medicine is for what. Some of what I know I learned from the massa, and some I learn myself from the Indians. When spring come, I tell you about my garden, but for now I just start with the jars. I got everything arranged," she said with a wave of her hand toward the neat shelves. "That purple herb is what the Indians call foxglove. That's for a bad heart. The green plant is hellebore—that's for high blood pressure." On her table was a plant with greenish white blossoms. "That's golden seal. It's for sores that won't heal."

Theresa shook her head. Pammy sighed. "I'll tell you the names first and later tell you what they're for." She spent the afternoon pointing to jars and getting Theresa to repeat the strange names. By the time the light began to fade, Theresa could identify a dozen herbs by color, texture, and smell. When it was dark, Pammy led her back to the kitchen where the house slaves were assembling for their evening meal. After Moses served the McIntyres, he presided over the table in the kitchen. Dicey sat at the other end, with Pammy and Puss on either side. Two women Theresa learned were sisters, Hetty and Letty, who did the heavy housework for Mrs. McIntyre, were also at the table, as were the coachman, Brutus, and the head gardener, Amos.

Theresa was too busy eating to worry that she could not understand their conversation. When she had finished, she was overcome with such weariness that she could not hold her head up. She let it slip forward to rest on the table. "This gal's tuckered," said Dicey. "Letty, you take her to Missus."

Theresa dragged herself slowly to her feet and followed Letty down the breezeway to the house, carrying the rest of her new clothes. Mrs. McIntyre was alone in her sitting room. Without a word, she took a candle and led Theresa up two flights of stairs to an attic crowded with strange shapes whose outlines Theresa could barely make out by the light of the candle. Mrs. McIntyre led her to a tiny room with a bed, washstand, and pegs on the wall for her clothes. "Don't waste the candle," said Mrs. McIntyre, and left her.

Theresa put on her shift and fell into her bed. Although her body ached with fatigue, she could not go to sleep at once. Her mind was too crowded with new impressions, and it was the first time in her entire life that she had slept by herself. For years she had slept in the large bed with her parents, and then she and her sister Claire had moved into a small room of their own. On board the *Dolphin*, the Acadians had huddled together for warmth and reassurance. Here she was, in a solitary bed, in a strange country, quite alone. Had her family found a new home? Had little Evariste and Richard survived the journey? Evariste had always been such a delicate child. She thought of the children and babies who had died on the *Dolphin* and shuddered. And where was Philippe? "Oh, God, spare Philippe," she said. "Spare Philippe," she whispered again as she drifted off to sleep.

The next few weeks were filled with strange new experiences for Theresa. She gradually began to pick up more English, and although she rarely saw her master and mistress, she came to know their slaves as people. She was particularly fond of Moses, and she could tell that he liked her, too. Most of her time she spent in the dispensary with Pammy. She learned the simpler remedies first: tartar emetic for constipation, ipecac to induce vomiting, linseed oil for congestion, oil of juniper for pains in the chest. Alfalfa tea eased the pains of arthritis; lobelia cured asthma. She soon knew that camomile tea cured insomnia, calomel tea indigestion, and sassafras tea reduced fever. The sap of the pine tree soothed boils; decoctions of sumac, yellow root, and juniper berries were good diuretics. A mixture of sulfur and lard was used to reduce itching. Besides foxglove, she learned other cardiac stimulants: horsemint, Virginia poke, Irish morning glory, an infusion of holly. Pammy made her own cough syrup from a mixture of clover, mullein, wild cherry bark, and white pine twigs. A poultice for the relief of hemorrhoids was produced by simmering the roots and leaves of cranesbill, privet, yarrow, and loosestrife in hot water. For hysteria, Dr. McIntyre gave his patients one dram each of opium, castor, saffron, and maple seed. The sick flocked from the far reaches of Talbot County to receive Pammy's cures, paying in eggs, a chicken, or a bit of tobacco. There was very little currency in the colony, and tobacco could be used to pay any debt.

Theresa soon settled into a routine that was broken only on Sunday when she was taken to church by Mrs. McIntyre. Her mistress carried a small silver warming pan full of hot coals on which she placed her feet to keep warm during the long service, but servants were permitted no such luxuries, and Theresa sat with chattering teeth in the cold church, her cloak pulled tightly around her.

The minister's sermons seemed interminable, and as Theresa sat listening to words she could barely understand, she could not help comparing Sundays in Maryland with those in Acadia. At that time of year in Grand Pré, the Landrys would all be bundled for the ride, and steam would rise from the flanks of her father's horse as he pulled the cart bearing them to the Church of St. Charles. The services were much shorter that the ones she was forced to attend in Maryland, and many of the men would deposit their wives and children and go outside where they joked and talked while their families heard mass. On a few occasions, they had even raced their horses around the church during the service. Sometimes the men would become so noisy that the priest would have to scold them. In Maryland, religion was clearly a much more serious matter. The parishioners sat with long faces while being told that most of them were doomed to hell, and a proctor held a long pole with which he struck those who went to sleep or seemed insufficiently attentive.

Theresa was not made to work on Sunday afternoon, but she found that her idleness, although intended as a welcome respite from her labors, only inclined her to gloomy thoughts of her lost home and family. She remembered the sights and smells of her childhood haunts with the greatest clarity, and they would rise before her while she sat in Mrs. McIntyre's sitting room, listening to the ticking of the clock. Her favorite childhood memory was of one afternoon when her father had taken her with him when he went to inspect his section of the dike. She could not have been more than five years old. Her father had pulled her up behind him, and she had ridden with her arms around him. He had kept his horse at a slow walk so that she would not fall off and had talked to her of adult matters, which she did not understand. She had nodded her head wisely as if she knew what he meant. Someday she would understand, someday when she was older, she knew.

Most often she missed Philippe. She would bury her face in her hands and conjure up his image. Once again, she saw his fine features and beautiful body and the deep brown eyes that melted when he looked at her. Once again, in her imagination, he came toward her with his jaunty, self-assured swagger, his auburn hair gleaming red in the sun, and she recalled how she pretended to be angry at his affectionate teasing and laughed at his jokes. She remembered the first time they had made love, two days after her father had forbidden them to marry, and she wanted him so desperately that she was sick with longing.

As sorely as she missed her father, there were times when she hated him. If he had only been reasonable, she and Philippe would be married now, together in exile. She could bear anything if only she had Philippe. She hated the heavy silence of the McIntyre household and the dour look of disapproval with which Mrs. McIntyre greeted the world. Dr. McIntyre was often away, and he never paid any attention to her at all. Until, that is, a snowy night in December, when Theresa had been in the McIntyre home for almost a month.

Chapter Nine

On a blustering winter night shortly before Christmas, Dr.
McIntyre came home much the worse for drink. It was a
Wednesday, and Mrs. McIntyre had gone to prayer meeting
at the church. Theresa's master threw himself into a chair
before the fire with a heavy sigh and stared at the flames as if
hypnotized. "Would you like something to eat and drink?"
Theresa asked.

"No, I just want to take the chill off, Theresa. You could
help me with my boots."

Theresa bent and tugged with all her might to remove the
doctor's mud-stained boots. He pushed his hands against her
shoulders and laughed as she fell back with a thud, his boot in
her hand. Dr. McIntyre helped her to her feet.

"It's a wild night out," he said. "We'll have a white
Christmas this year."

"Yes, sir," Theresa replied. The doctor did not seem to
want anything, but he had not given her permission to leave.
"Can I get you anything?" she repeated.

"Nay, lass, just sit with me by the fire and keep me
company for a while."

He had never required that of her, and the request made her
uncomfortable, but she complied. He sat staring at the flames

and spoke at last. "I'm a lonely man, Theresa. There's no greater curse than an unhappy marriage, but you've no doubt observed that for yourself. I should never have married Elizabeth. It was a mismatch from the very beginning. I was away from home for the first time, studying medicine in Edinburgh. I was lonely, and Elizabeth was easy to talk to. I thought she understood me. Now I think that I did most of the talking and she just sat and listened. I'm not the kind of man she wanted, either—she would have been happier with some Bible-thumping minister—but she was twenty-four and had no prospects when I met her."

Theresa had no desire to be taken into the doctor's confidence, but she had no choice but to listen, so she sat down in a chair and folded her hands in her lap.

"After a while, marriage just seemed like the natural thing to do; not that we courted that long, mind you. If we had, we might have thought better of it, both of us. It didn't seem to matter so much earlier, but now I'm feeling my age, and it saddens me to think of all the wasted years. You'll be thinking of marriage yourself someday. Take a word of advice from one who's suffered and don't enter into marriage hastily."

Dr. McIntyre gave Theresa a lugubrious look through drink-reddened eyes. "Come a little closer, Theresa," he said, patting his knee. "You're too far away."

Theresa was now alarmed and tried to calculate how long it would be before the return of Mrs. McIntyre. Until then, she would be alone in the house with her master. She rose and tried to keep her voice calm. "I'm sorry, sir, but I have work to do, if you'll excuse me."

She turned and tried to leave the room, but Dr. McIntyre reached out and grasped her arm. "Don't leave, Theresa. You don't know what it's like to be lonely. You're such a sweet young thing—help me keep these old bones warm." He pulled her to him and gave her a wet kiss that tasted of stale liquor. "The Missus will never know," he whispered. "It will be our little secret, just between the two of us."

Theresa beat the doctor's chest with her hands and struggled from side to side until she broke his grip. Had he been sober, she would never have escaped, but he stumbled as he pursued her. She backed slowly away from him toward the fire until she could feel its heat searing her back. Reaching behind her, she grasped an iron poker and managed to lift it above her head just as the doctor lunged and grabbed her arm again.

Theresa was in a panic. If she were going to strike, she would have to do so now. Did she dare to hit her master? What would he do to her afterward? What would she say to Mrs. McIntyre? Would her mistress believe that his advances had been unprovoked, or would she perhaps think that Theresa had encouraged him and then changed her mind at the last minute?

The door burst open, and there stood Mrs. McIntyre. "Edmund, might I ask what you are doing?"

Dr. McIntyre wheeled around to face his wife. "It was her fault," he said thickly. "She lured me, flaunting her breasts like a hussy. She always entices me," he ended lamely, stopped short by the look on Mrs. McIntyre's face.

"Yes, I can see how she is enticing you, with a poker held over her head," said Mrs. McIntyre in tones of such contempt and loathing that Theresa shivered. Until that moment, she had stood there frozen, the poker raised over her head, but at last she lowered it slowly and replaced it in the andiron rack.

"I'm sorry," said Dr. McIntyre with a whine in his voice. "It's the drink, Elizabeth. I'm a weak man when I've had a drop too much."

"No, Edmund. You have a drop too much because you're a weak man. You may go to bed, Theresa."

Theresa darted out of the door as soon as she was given permission and went straight to her room, where she lay down and attempted to still her thudding heart. Even worse than the narrowness of her escape was her certainty that sooner or later Dr. McIntyre would force his attentions on her again; she might not escape as easily a second time.

The arrival of Christmas made little difference in the McIntyre household. There were no festivities and no decorations, but the slaves had the day off and received gifts. Theresa, who had been given the equivalent of a servant's entire wardrobe upon her arrival, received nothing but her share of the Christmas dinner.

On Christmas afternoon, she received a visit from Leon. They were allowed to see each other in the kitchen where Dicey fed him his second Christmas dinner of the day. Theresa hugged him in front of the slaves, which seemed to embarrass him, and demanded to know everything about his new home and position. He refused to speak of himself until he had looked about and satisfied himself that she was well situated. Leon had put on weight and was comfortably dressed in brown breeches, a coarse wool shirt, and a coat that he told her was a castoff from one of his new employers, the Ramseys. He had brought Theresa some candy from the Christmas celebration on the Ramsey plantation and told her that the Ramseys had had a great tree and presents, mostly clothing, for all the slaves and servants. There had been a grand celebration, with more food than Leon had ever seen before in one place, and no one had had to work for a day and a half.

"Perhaps the Ramseys will let me send for you next year," Leon said upon being told that Theresa had spent the morning in church. "Everyone should have a party once in a while."

"I don't think Protestants like parties. They seem to pray most of the time—when they're not working," said Theresa. "Mrs. McIntyre reads her Bible every night and says prayers before she goes to bed."

"Well, there are Protestants and Protestants," Leon replied. "The Ramseys don't pray more than necessary, and you never saw such folk for partying! Anything is an excuse for a ball. Of course, they are Church of England, not Presbyterian like the McIntyres."

Theresa did not know that there were different kinds of Protestants. She had assumed that Leon had fallen among much the same kind of folk as she had and was amazed at his account of the lavish parties the Ramseys gave for the gentry of Talbot County. He described as best he could the dances they did; their favorites were the minuet from France and a vigorous dance from England called the Roger de Coverley.

"When do they have time to work?"

"Oh, the Ramseys wouldn't dream of soiling their hands

with work! They're too fine for that by far! The men gamble and ride and talk politics, and the women lounge around discussing clothes and gossiping. They don't even take care of their own children. You'd think they were the laziest people on earth, but they can expend any amount of energy dancing till four in the morning."

"Mrs. McIntyre works as hard as Mother ever did, and Dr. McIntyre is gone all day mending people. Who takes care of the land?"

"Overseers and slaves and more servants than you've ever seen. Their plantation is as big as a whole town."

"And what are you doing, Leon?" Theresa asked.

"When they found out I was good with figures, they put me to work balancing their books. They were in a fine mess, I can tell you that. I've learned a lot from the ledgers about the way the plantation is run, and the waste is shocking. Caleb Wheeler is stealing them blind, and the slaves, of course, don't work any harder than they have to. The Ramseys have no idea what's going on under their noses. I have to walk a fine line, Theresa, not to make enemies. Wheeler has his eye on me all the time—he's afraid I'll tell the Ramseys what he's up to. He had no idea I was educated, or he'd never have hired me. I suppose he thought he was getting a free field hand, all brawn and no brain. I'll just have to be patient and bide my time. My day will come! As long as we're going to be here for a while, I might as well do what I can to advance myself."

At the conclusion of his visit, Theresa walked with Leon to the end of the square. "You haven't changed your mind about marrying me?" he asked as she turned to go.

"No, Leon, but thank you for asking. I know you mean well."

He sighed. "Let me know if you need anything. Good-bye, Theresa."

Theresa learned as much as she could from Pammy before the spring came. She would learn then how Pammy grew and cultivated her herbs and in the summer and autumn how they were dried and turned into medicines. Unless there was a heavy day at the dispensary, she was not needed there all of the time. When Pammy did not need her, Mrs. McIntyre brought her into the house to help Hetty and Letty with the cleaning. On her first day working in the house, she was given a feather duster and put to work in the bedrooms upstairs, dusting the posters of the beds and the heavy wardrobes and marble-topped washstands. After she had finished dusting, Mrs. McIntyre ran her finger over and under the surfaces of the furniture and made Theresa redo the spots she had missed. Mrs. McIntyre did not employ a housekeeper, as she preferred to supervise the running of her home herself, and she was a stern taskmistress. There were parquet floors and stone steps, oak paneling and fireplaces to be washed and buffed and polished. There were fires to be laid, and the ashes from the fires had to be collected to make strong lye soap of the kind with which Theresa had been scrubbed on her arrival. She was also set to work dipping tallow candles and occasionally given some sewing.

Theresa was the only white servant, and Mrs. McIntyre, who appeared to dislike and mistrust blacks, asked Theresa more and more often to sit with her at night. The doctor spent little of his time at home, and Theresa knew that Mrs. McIntyre was lonely. The two of them sewed in the sitting room, and Mrs. McIntyre would sometimes talk of her home and family in Scotland.

By the time she knew enough English to carry on simple conversations, Theresa understood that servants were treated like pieces of animated furniture. Although Mrs. McIntyre might, if she wished, confide in Theresa, she did not expect Theresa to confide her personal problems and opinions to Mrs. McIntyre. She was not, it seemed, even supposed to have any. Once, when Mrs. McIntyre spoke to Theresa of missing her home, Theresa said that she too was terribly homesick. That comment was met with such an icy stare that she never ventured such a remark again.

Late one afternoon, Theresa and Letty were scrubbing the front steps when Dr. McIntyre appeared at the corner on his horse, accompanying a woman in a carriage whose hair seemed unnaturally fair and bright to Theresa. They stopped at the corner for several minutes and appeared to be in deep conversation. The lady smiled and waved good-bye and then instructed her coachman to turn the carriage around and drive on. Dr. McIntyre cantered up the street and smiled at Theresa as he threw the reins of his horse to the groom who came out to greet him. "We won't tell Mrs. McIntyre about the lady, now, will we?" he said in a conspiratorial whisper.

"No, sir."

Theresa thought she saw the flutter of a curtain from an upstairs window, but she was not sure.

Theresa and Letty went back to their task, but ten minutes later they were summoned into the parlor by Mrs. McIntyre. She came to the point at once. "Theresa, what did the master say to you when he came home?"

"He asked how I am," she lied promptly, eyes downcast.

"Is that all?"

"Yes, ma'am."

"Did you see him talking to a young lady in a carriage?" Mrs. McIntyre stood up and strolled to the window.

"No, ma'am."

"Did you, Letty?"

Letty shot Theresa a guilty look. "I'm not sure, ma'am."

"Out with it, girl. You'll not be punished for telling the truth. I saw her clear as day with my own eyes. Now—did you see my husband in conversation with a young blonde lady?"

"Yes, ma'am," Letty replied.

"Did he ask Theresa not to mention this to me?"

Another guilty look in Theresa's direction. "Yes, ma'am."

"Very well, you may go. As for you, miss," she said to Theresa after Letty had left, "you may go to bed without your supper. Girls who lie are not fed."

The next morning, at breakfast, Letty related the incident to the other slaves and apologized to Theresa. "I'll get a beating if I lie," she said.

"I know," said Theresa. "I'm not angry with you. But what was I to do?"

"Stay out of their lives as much as you can," said Moses. "Lay low and don't never tell them more than you have to. Massa and Missus can do anything with us they want. We only got one thing—we know everything about them, and

70

they don't know anything about us. If you smart, you learn to blend into the woodwork.''

"But lately I seem to be with her half the time.''

"That don't matter. You can be there and not be there at the same time. You got to play dumb—the dumber we are, the more they like us. Never volunteer nothing. Pretend you don't understand nothing that's going on around you. How you think I got to be head nigger around this place? Moses never hear nothing, never see nothing, never know nothing. As far as Massa concern, I just a poor woolly-head fool.'' Moses rolled his eyes and put on a face of such abject stupidity that Theresa had to laugh.

"Who was that woman with the doctor?'' she asked after her giggling fit subsided.

"Her hair yellow or brown?''

"Yellow.''

"That be Roger Caffery's wife. The one with brown hair be Cecilia Hathaway. Them's the only two he keeps company with right now, unless he got a new one I ain't heard about yet. That one thing you can say for sure about Massa—he sure like to have a good time with a pretty lady.''

"Why didn't he marry one?''

"Because the Missus have plenty of money. How that marriage come about happen this way. When old Master Edmund be alive, he send young Master Edmund all the way to Edinburgh to the best doctor school in Scotland. While the young master away, the old master die, and we told that there ain't nothing left but debts and we all got to be sold. You talk about one bunch of scared niggers! Then, out of nowhere, we hear that all the debts been paid and we ain't got a thing to worry about. The next year, Massa Edmund come home from Scotland with the Missus. Skinny bride, fat purse, that's what all of us say about her.''

The other slaves nodded. It was a tale with which they were all familiar.

'I got to go serve breakfast, but there something else I got to tell you before I go. Don't ever trust Massa or Missus, no matter how nice they are to you. And if you want something from them, they'll give it to you if you can make them think the idea came from them. And one more thing—if they give you something, act like you real happy whether you want it or not. They love to think that we love them.''

One night, not long after this event, Dr. McIntyre was late for dinner. Mrs. McIntyre awaited his arrival in the front parlor with ill-concealed impatience, pacing the room with her hands clasped and stopping occasionally to rearrange the ornaments on the mantel or fuss with the room's furnishings. She had insisted that Theresa sit with her. At the sound of a horse or carriage clattering down the street, she would rush to the window and look out, then drop the heavy drapes and stand staring moodily into space.

"He didn't come in at all last night," she whined.

Theresa had learned that news at breakfast, but remained silent, remembering Moses' advice. When Moses announced dinner, Mrs. McIntyre snapped that she would wait for the master, and the black man withdrew, leaving his mistress to resume her pacing. When they heard Dr. McIntyre at last, Theresa rose to leave, but Mrs. McIntyre detained her with a motion of her hand. The doctor came in blustering and voluble and tried to kiss his wife but refused to look her in the eye. Mrs. McIntyre turned her face away and stared at him accusingly until his speech trailed off into a lame silence.

"We agreed I was not to be publicly humiliated," she said at last, her voice full of suppressed fury. "That was our bargain."

"You may leave, Theresa," said Dr. McIntyre, casting a look of warning at his wife.

"Stay where you are," Mrs. McIntyre snapped. "Why not speak in front of the servants? Do you think there is anyone in this house—or in this town, for that matter—who doesn't know you didn't come home last night? Do you think our names aren't on the lips of every barmaid and tavern brawler in Oxford, not to mention respectable folk?''

"I'm sorry, Elizabeth. What else can I say?" said Dr. McIntyre with an ineffectual shrug of his shoulders.

"I suppose I'm to believe that you were with a patient last night," she said, her voice heavy with sarcasm.

"No, I won't lie. I'd been drinking, and I know you don't like to see me in that condition, so I didn't come home. I slept it off at Duffy's Tavern, and that's God's truth.''

"And what's that to stay away from home for? When do I see you without the reek of spirits on your breath?"

"Ah, Lizzy, you're a hard one. I don't mean I'd stopped for a pint. I mean I wasn't sober! It's not the same!"

"You're an intemperate man, Edmund McIntyre, and a lecher to boot, and I rue the day we wed!"

Her husband caught her by the shoulders and once again tried to kiss her, but once again she turned away. "Don't say that, Lizzy, not after all this time," he said in a low voice.

"It's true. I knew you for what you were when I married you, and God has punished us both," she cried.

"You'll not start that again!" the doctor yelled back.

"It's true! If we were better folk, he wouldn't have taken all the bairns from us!"

"You mustn't think that way. There's nothing to be gained by dwelling on the past. It was God's will. Come, now, we'll have a bite to eat, and we'll forget it. You're overwrought—I wish you'd take a bit of brandy."

"That I will not. One drunkard in the family is enough."

He sighed and led her toward the dining room, leaving Theresa in her corner. They had both apparently forgotten her existence. She had understood most of their conversation, but she would have to ask Moses or Letty what "lecher" and "bairns" meant and why Mrs. McIntyre thought she was being punished.

At supper, she related what she could of the McIntyres' exchange. "That an old story," said Moses with a sigh. "They been saying the same things to each other for years."

"What's a 'lecher'?"

"That be a man who do with other women what he only supposed to do with his wife." The other slaves laughed.

"And 'bairns'?" Theresa asked.

"Bairns be children. The master and missus had five children, two girls and three boys, and they all died. Missy Mary and Master Robert live the longest, for about five years. Lord, when Master Robert died, that be a bad time! I thought the missus go clean off her head with grief. There ain't no happiness in this home since that day. Massa stay away more and more; Missus all time reading the Good Book."

Late that night, Theresa was awakened from a sound sleep

to find Mrs. McIntyre shaking her shoulder. "Theresa, wake up."

"What's wrong?" Theresa asked sleepily, shaking her head to clear it.

"I need some company. Come downstairs with me."

Theresa dutifully struggled out of her warm bed, put on her shoes, and descended the stairs behind Mrs. McIntyre, who was trembling so that the shadow cast by her candle danced crazily on the wall. Downstairs in her sitting room, Mrs. McIntyre lit two oil lamps and started the fire that had been laid for the next day. Then she sank into her rocking chair and burst into tears.

"Whatever is the matter?" cried Theresa, who had never seen her mistress so distressed.

Mrs. McIntyre rocked back and forth, back and forth, her frame racked with sobs. "I had the dream again," she said when she could speak. "Why won't it go away? Always the same. I hear my babies crying, and I wake up and get out of bed, and . . . all dead, all dead. Oh, God, I wish I had been barren rather than lose so many."

"Yes, it is a terrible thing to hear a sick child cry." Theresa started to tell Mrs. McIntyre of the deaths of her friends' children on board the *Dolphin*, but she checked herself in time.

"Robert died of diphtheria. At the end, his throat closed. Nothing would go down it, and he begged and begged for water. Poor little bairn, how he suffered from thirst! How they all cry to me from the grave! Cursed," she muttered, staring at Theresa through reddened eyes. "God has cursed this union. Yet, yet . . . I know that my Redeemer liveth, and on the final day my bairns shall rise again, with new bodies. 'And many of them that sleep in the dust of the earth shall awake, some to everlasting life, and some to shame and everlasting contempt.' The Book of Daniel, chapter twelve, verse two."

She was calmer now and stopped her rocking. "I'll be fine. I just didn't want to be alone. You go on back to bed—you need your sleep."

"Are you sure you're all right?"

"Yes. Go on back to bed."

The next day, Mrs. McIntyre was pale as death, with large black rings under her eyes, and she snapped at Theresa and the slaves so viciously that they did everything in their power to stay out of her way.

Chapter Ten

For several months, Dr. McIntyre made no further attempt to force his attentions on Theresa. She knew from the slaves' gossip that he was often in the company of the two women— Roger Caffery's wife and the widow Cecilia Hathaway—and she could only hope that those women would divert his attention. Still, she watched her master anxiously and carefully and made her manner with him as impersonal as possible when she was forced to speak to him. She noticed that his drinking was growing steadily worse—a fine tremor shook his hands, and his absences from home were more frequent. The broken veins in his face and his puffy, bloodshot eyes were more noticeable than ever, and his expanding belly led him to curse and snarl that his clothes were too tight. She did not know why, but Theresa knew that he was degenerating rapidly. She feared that the wounds to his vanity would eventually cause him to turn against her once again.

"Massa's ladies show him the door," Moses announced one night over dinner in the kitchen. "Roger Caffery's wife was only using him to make her husband jealous, and that old widow Hathaway done caught her another husband."

"Oh, Lord," said Hetty with a resigned sigh. "I reckon he be bothering one of us again."

"He getting so old and fat, I don't think he going to be bothering women at all much longer," said Letty.

"A man who's as stuck on himself as Massa will go to the grave bothering women, if only to prove he can," Hetty replied. "He sure loves to think he's one big devil with the ladies!"

"Women ain't his only problem," Moses said. "He's been losing money gambling again. I don't know where that will lead to if he gets bad in debt again."

Theresa absorbed the news in silence and finished her meal. But that very night she heard the steps up to her attic room creaking slowly. She knew from the tread that it was her master's and from the stealthy way he placed each foot on the stairs that he was trying to keep from waking his wife. Alarmed, she sat up in bed with the blanket pulled up to her chin, her mind racing as she thought of a way to stall him.

The doctor came stumbling into her little room without knocking, reeking of whiskey, and sat down beside her. "Theresa," he said thickly, his trembling fingers caressing the dark curls tumbling down her back. Then his hand fell almost casually to rest on one of her swelling breasts. "Such a pretty girl, so warm and sweet. Not like other women, cold, grasping witches . . ." His voice, filled with self-pity, trailed off, and he stared at Theresa through drink-reddened eyes.

"Gimme a kiss," he said, slurring his words. "Just a kiss to comfort an old man." He leaned forward and planted a wet kiss on her mouth. It took all of her willpower to keep from turning her head aside and pushing him roughly off her bed, but Theresa knew that physical force would not save her.

She spotted a whiskey flask tucked beneath the folds of Dr. McIntyre's nightshirt, and it gave her an idea. "Let's have a drink," she said, forcing herself to smile.

"Good idea," he said, twisting the top off the silver flask. "Li'l drink to cheer us up." He turned the flask back and took a deep swallow, then wiped his mouth and handed the flask to Theresa. She took a deep breath and closed her lips against the mouth of the flask, turning it back and pretending to drink. She gasped and choked as a thin trickle of the potent liquid escaped from the flask and made its way down her throat. The doctor pounded her on the back as she coughed.

"Sweet thing, not a drinker, are you? You'll get used to it soon enough. Here, I'll show you." He took the flask from her and took another deep swallow, then handed it back to her. This time Theresa took a small sip and found that the burning liquid did produce a warm, glowing sensation in her throat and stomach.

"Is something troubling you?" she asked after a few moments.

"Damned women. False, worthless. Not true as they should be—tell you anything to get what they want. I'll bet you're a sweet, simple girl, Theresa. Girls should be simple—who needs a shrewd, conniving female? Shouldn't be taught to read, blast 'em."

"Have another drink and tell me all about it," Theresa said in a voice dripping with honey. "Poor Dr. McIntyre."

"Call me Edmund," he said after he had taken another deep drink. "Thass my name. No need for formality between friends. You are my friend, aren't you?"

"Of course," she said. "Have another little drink. It will make you feel better."

He drank again. "That's not what I need to make me feel better," he said, tossing the nearly empty flask aside. A thin stream of liquor escaped and left a trail on the floor. "Kiss me, Theresa," the doctor muttered, once again planting wet lips on hers. This time both of his hands went to her breasts and then moved to lift her gown. Theresa tensed herself, forcing herself to endure his caresses. As his hands moved up her naked flesh, she could only pray that the liquor would do its work. Dr. McIntyre pushed her back onto her bed, and just as he had begun fumbling beneath his own nightshirt, he exhaled a long sigh, gave a short snore, and toppled over, unconscious.

Limp with relief, Theresa closed her eyes and crept from the bed. She covered the doctor with her blanket and made a small bed for herself out of blankets near the door.

The next morning, Theresa tried to slip out of the room without disturbing Dr. McIntyre, who was snoring with his mouth wide open, but as she finished dressing, he sat up in bed, groaning and mumbling and holding his head.

"Oh God, where's Moses? Tell him to bring me my coffee."

"Have you forgotten where you are?" Theresa said in her sweetest voice. As the doctor looked around and became gradually aware of his surroundings, the events of the evening slowly came back to him.

"Have I? Did we . . . ?" His voice trailed off, and he looked at Theresa helplessly.

She lowered her eyes, blushed, and did her best to look coy and girlish.

"Well, heh, heh, heh . . ." he laughed, pulling down his nightshirt and rising with a bit of a swagger. "I'd best be slipping downstairs before the missus wakes up, hadn't I?" He gave Theresa a conspiratorial wink and, collecting his flask, left and tiptoed cautiously down the stairs.

Theresa sank to her bed, weak and trembling. She did not know how in the world she was to handle him next time, but at least she had obtained a reprieve.

With the approach of spring, Theresa was told by Pammy how they would plant herbs and exactly when each had to be gathered. She learned to prepare infusions, like tea, which were steeped, then removed, and decoctions, in which the herbs themselves were used in the medicine after having been boiled for several minutes.

Theresa also learned from the constant stream of humanity at the dispensary door. People came complaining of every conceivable human misery but also told Pammy a great deal about their lives and families. Some of them, believing the black woman to have magic powers, would ask for potions to restore their husbands' affections, and one woman even carried her dead child for miles through a driving rain to ask Pammy if she could breathe life into the corpse.

Pammy was frequently called upon by women for a painkilling remedy for menstrual cramps, and she was also asked, in terrified whispers, for her secret tonic that prevented conception. Pammy passed this formula on to Theresa after extracting a solemn oath that she would never reveal the secret to anyone except her own future students. Very soon, Theresa knew almost as much as Pammy and could have taken over the running of the dispensary had it been necessary.

She was learning to manipulate the McIntyres through their

79

weaknesses, and she gradually developed the conviction that it was she who was the adult and they who were the children. She felt a sense of superiority to her masters, which she discovered she shared with their slaves. The McIntyres could afford to be vain and self-indulgent and to lose their tempers, but their servants could not.

Her greatest difficulty was a crushing loneliness that was relieved only by the relationships she formed with the household slaves and by Leon's visits, which became more frequent as his position at the Ramsey plantation improved.

Leon's first opportunity to advance himself came soon after his arrival. Throughout his first winter, he observed smoke rising from fires that had been set to clear new land. When he asked Caleb Wheeler what the new land was to be used for, Wheeler replied, "To plant tobacco, of course."

"Do you plan to purchase new slaves?" Leon asked. He did not see how new land could be cultivated without more hands.

"No, stupid. The old land is wore out," Wheeler replied with a sneer, "so we don't need 'em."

Wheeler was barely literate himself, and Leon's book learning and quiet competence had posed a threat to the overseer from the beginning. Moreover, Wheeler lived in constant fear of having his dishonesty exposed, but he bullied Leon whenever he could.

"Worn out? You mean you keep having to clear new land to plant tobacco?"

"You don't know as much as you thought you did, do you, Frenchy? Everyone knows tobacco is a hard crop. It wears soil out fast."

"Have you ever thought of trying to do anything about that?"

"Nothing you can do about it except to clear new land."

"But—what a waste!"

Wheeler shrugged. "What of it? If there's one thing we got plenty of, it's land. Besides, clearing new land keeps the niggers occupied in the winter."

Leon pondered this conversation for a long time. He remembered reading once that the German farmers of Pennsylvania rotated their crops to avoid the exhaustion of their soil.

That had not been necessary in Nova Scotia, and Leon had not paid a great deal of attention to what he read. He could only remember that some crops were harder on soil than others and that the German farmers divided their fields into threes. A crop that exhausted the soil was planted in one field, and two different crops, on the others. He wished he could remember the details. As he talked to Wheeler and some of the slaves responsible for the cultivation of tobacco, a plan formed slowly in his mind. He knew better than to suggest it to Wheeler. In addition to his dislike of Leon, Wheeler was a rigid man, set in his ways and afraid of change.

Leon related the story to Theresa during a visit in early spring. He would bide his time, he explained, until the opportunity presented itself for him to talk to the member of the Ramsey family he had singled out as being the most responsible. The head of the Ramsey family, Horace Ramsey, was a retiring, scholarly man who spent most of his time in his library. The oldest son, Everett, was wild and headstrong, too involved in gambling and siring mulatto children to be concerned with managing his land. It was the second son, Nathaniel, whom Leon decided to approach.

Nathaniel had recently concluded his formal education with a grand tour of Europe and upon his return had taken more interest in the daily operations of the plantation than the rest of the family put together. It was Nathaniel who checked on Leon during the first months he had spent trying to straighten out the plantation ledgers. He made no comment on Leon's work but would raise his eyebrows at the confusion and give Leon an occasional nod of approval as the snarl was gradually untangled.

In late March, shortly before the time when the tobacco seedlings were transplanted to the fields, Leon took Nathaniel Ramsey aside and cautiously raised the subject of the land wastage caused by the periodic exhaustion of the soil.

"Yes, it's a shame," Nathaniel agreed. "Not only is it time consuming and inefficient, but a lot of timber is burned simply to get it out of the way. I wish there were something we could do about it."

"There may be." Leon told Nathaniel of what he had read.

81

"I was thinking, sir, that with your permission I might try a similar experiment here."

"Crop rotation. Hmm, it sounds intriguing. I'm just beginning to realize how little I know about growing tobacco. Unfortunately, Greek and Latin and mathematics did little to prepare me to take over here, but someone's got to do it. On my return from Europe, I suddenly became aware of how inefficiently this place is managed. What other crops besides tobacco would you plant?"

Leon had given this subject considerable thought. His experience in Acadia had prepared him to grow wheat and raise cattle, and he could only hope that wheat would be a good crop to rotate with tobacco. He could not, as it happened, have made a more felicitous choice, as wheat restored to the soil the nitrogen that tobacco removed. He would plant a third field in clover for the livestock. Nathaniel listened carefully to his proposal and, over the strenuous objections of Caleb Wheeler, authorized the use of three small fields and sufficient manpower for Leon's experiment.

Across the river, Theresa knew that it was only a matter of time until she would hear the creak of Dr. McIntyre's step on the stairs one night. His behavior puzzled her at first. He would wink at her when he came home at night and occasionally make a feeble attempt at flirtation, but then he would ignore her entirely for days on end. She came to believe with the slaves that he had reached a stage where he only approached women out of habit and the desire to salve his vanity—it seemed to have little to do with any geniuine physical need. Theresa was thankful she deceived him into thinking he had conquered her, and the doctor seemed willing enough to enter into the deception.

At last, the dreaded night came. He came tiptoeing into her room, smelling of whiskey but not drunk. He was much steadier this time, and even the trembling of his hands seemed to have stopped temporarily.

Theresa had been thinking ever since his first trip to her room how she was to handle him on the next occasion. Moses had made several references to Dr. McIntyre's gambling debts and to imprudent investments and other financial difficulties

82

in which their master was embroiled, and it had given her an idea. When he sat down heavily on the side of her bed and began fumbling for her, she clenched her fists and buried her head in his chest.

"Oh, Edmund," she sighed, "I can't bear stealing moments in this dreary attic. Wouldn't it be lovely if we had a place of our own?"

He stopped his fumbling abruptly and looked down at her. "Did you say a place of our own?"

Theresa gave him the smile that she knew brought deep dimples to her cheeks and looked up at him through her thick curly lashes. "Oh, yes," she sighed. "I've done nothing but think about you since the last time you were here, but I just can't bear seeing you in this dreary old place. I think we both deserve something better. My father was a rich man in Acadia, and it's not right that I should be treated like a slave."

"A place of our own," Dr. McIntyre repeated, rubbing his chin thoughtfully. He had only the haziest recollection of having visited Theresa before, but apparently whatever had transpired had made a deep impression on the girl. She was obviously smitten with him, and why should she not be? He was, after all, a man of the world, and she, a simple peasant. If he set her up in a little place, he would have somewhere to retire to when he was drinking or simply wanted to avoid his wife's nagging. Elizabeth would nag and scold, but Theresa would be worth every minute of it. He could even meet his friends there for a card game or two. A place of his own where he could relax at the end of a hard day. . . . Yes, why hadn't he thought of it himself? Everyone in town would know he was keeping a pretty wench, and he would no longer be dependent on the favor of vain, rich women who were difficult to please. He was, he had to admit to himself, beginning to feel his age, and the physical demands of knowing women had begun to tire him. His drinking had certainly not helped him in that quarter. No one need know what transpired between Theresa and himself. She would be easily satisfied with a few decent dresses and trinkets and whatever affection he felt like bestowing on her from time to time. It was an excellent idea. There was only one problem. . . .

"I couldn't do it at once," he said, thinking aloud. "Your

place would have to be furnished decently, and you would need some sort of carriage and a servant or two. But it is a good idea."

"I thought you were a rich man," Theresa said, pouting prettily and twisting the ruffle of his nightshirt around her finger.

"I am, of course, a man of means," he said, puffing out his chest, "but I have made some unwise investments and am temporarily embarrassed. Only temporarily embarrassed, I assure you," he added hastily. "I'm sure I can see my way to setting you up before long." So engrossed in this new idea was he, that he picked up his candle and left her without another word.

Theresa lay back on her pillow and breathed a sigh of relief. Once again, her wits had saved her. She had no idea what she would do when and if he did decide to set her up in a place of her own, but she was learning to live life one day at a time and solve her problems as they arose. She laughed at her conniving mind. What a deceitful little baggage she had become! But what choice did she have? She had no intentions of submitting to Dr. McIntyre unless it was absolutely necessary, and she had nothing but her brains to save her.

Suddenly, Theresa thought of her family and Philippe and sighed. Where were her parents, her brothers and sisters? More important, where was Philippe? She must cling to the hope that somehow they would be reunited. She could not bear to think of a future without Philippe.

Chapter Eleven

In addition to their town property, the McIntyres owned a modest farm a short distance from Oxford where they raised livestock and grew some produce and a little tobacco. On a day in late April, Theresa was instructed to go to the farm and pluck two geese. Goose feathers were too highly prized as stuffing for mattresses and pillows to wait until the birds were killed to pluck them; their feathers were removed in the spring before their summer moulting. Theresa approached this task with considerable trepidation, as her experience with geese had taught her that they were foul-tempered creatures; she was sure they would not take kindly to being deprived of their feathers. She was given a small woven basket to put over their heads to keep them from pecking her. Theresa tucked her hair up under a linen cap and donned a long apron that completely covered her dress. Thus protected, she set out after her morning's work in the dispensary.

The day was brilliant and unseasonably cool, the air clear and invigorating, and as she walked along with her cloak drawn about her against the chill, she hummed fragments of a song her mother had taught her. Tiny wisps of cloud floated in a bright blue sky, and in spite of the unpleasant nature of her errand, Theresa's spirits rose.

Once in the McIntyres' barnyard, she decided to go for the older, slower goose first. She managed to surprise the fowl from behind, trapping it between her knees and slipping the basket over its head in one deft motion. While the goose was still confused, she got it into a bin in the barn, and despite its strenuous vocal protests, she soon had it as naked as the day it was born. The first half of her task completed, Theresa sat down to rest for a moment with a cold dipper of water from the well, pleased that she had done so well. She was covered with tiny feathers, and her hands and lower arms had been pricked by quills, but it had not been as difficult as she expected.

The second goose was another matter entirely. Not only was she younger and swifter, but she had been alerted by the raucous honking from within the barn that some mischief was afoot. When Theresa emerged, preceded by her enraged and naked victim, the second goose eyed Theresa with the gravest suspicion and began waddling rapidly around the enclosure. Theresa chased her for half an hour in vain. At last, the goose flew into the barn and wedged herself tightly between two posts. Theresa's attempts to hood her met with such vicious pecking that Theresa's arms were cut and bruised.

"Here goosey, nice goosey," she crooned, attempting one last time to coax the animal. In reply, the goose hissed malevolently and sat switching her tail feathers from side to side, regarding Theresa with singular disfavor all the while. At last, Theresa sat down in the cool barn hay, only temporarily discouraged, to plot a new strategy.

She was startled by a sound behind her. Turning, she saw a man's form framed in the barn door. Her eyes had grown accustomed to the dark interior of the barn, and she could see nothing but the man's silhouette framed against the bright light outside. She shaded her eyes with her hand, peering. "Who's there?" For some reason, her heart began pounding.

"Theresa—is it you?" The figure took a step closer.

"Philippe," she whispered. "My God, Philippe, you've come for me." She could still not see him clearly, but there was only one man in the whole world who sounded like that. He had the same lithe, springy step, the same beautiful, lean-hipped body she remembered so well. And he was running toward her right now!

Theresa's knees were suddenly so weak that she could not rise. Philippe sank to his knees beside her and cupped her face in his hands, staring at it as if he had never seen it before. Then he put his arms around her and crushed her to him with such force that she lost her breath. "I knew you'd come for me if I waited long enough," she said as soon as she could speak.

"Of course I came for you. Did you doubt me?" he said, his voice rising, muffled, from her hair.

"No, not for an instant." She buried her face in his shoulder, and they held each other for a long moment. He was thinner—she could feel his ribs beneath his shirt. But his long, slender neck, with the auburn hair growing gracefully into its hollow, was so dear and so familiar that she could hardly hold back tears of joy. His smooth skin was the same; his scent was the same. It was like being home again. He was so handsome that it hurt her to look at him.

"Don't cry," he said, kissing the single tear that fell on her cheek. "Don't cry, Theresa." They sank onto the hay, still in each other's arms.

Philippe took off her cap, and a mass of black curls cascaded down her back. He picked up a handful of her hair and buried his face in it. "My God, I'd forgotten how beautiful you are." He took both her hands and pressed them to his lips, whispering her name.

Theresa shuddered and closed her eyes. She felt as if a dam were bursting, sweeping her away in a long-suppressed flood of emotion.

"Philippe, I've been so lonely, so lonely that I wanted to die. I never dreamed it could hurt so much."

"I know the feeling." He pulled her face to his and gave her a long, lingering kiss.

Slowly, gently, they fell back into the fragrant hay. Theresa unbuttoned his coarse shirt and traced with wonder the hard, compact contours of his body.

"Theresa, I love you so much." Philippe's voice was hoarse with longing.

His hands were everywhere, turning her blood to fire. He

untied her apron, and she helped him with the long row of buttons down the front of her dress. They fumbled with each other's clothing, frantic in their haste, like two young animals.

Afterward, they lay touching each other's bodies, laughing at the bits of hay that stuck in their hair. But, inevitably, Theresa was soon full of questions that demanded immediate replies.

"Oh, Philippe, where have you been?"

"I've been looking for you for six months, searching for you everywhere. I combed every inch of the northern colonies and then worked my way south. It hasn't been easy, but that's all behind me now. It doesn't matter. Nothing matters except that I've found you."

"Where were you sent?"

"Nowhere. I was put on a ship called the *Pembroke*, and we mutinied not long after we left and went back to Grand Pré. I took care of that bastard Winslow and then came looking for you. I have no idea where the *Pembroke* was supposed to go; they wouldn't tell us." Philippe sat up and put an arm around Theresa.

"I tried to get on your ship. I almost drowned getting on the *Dolphin*, and then you weren't there," she said sadly.

"I knew you'd do something like that. They separated the men that escaped and put us on different ships. I did everything I could to get word to you."

"I know you did. But Philippe, nothing matters now that we're together again."

"Have you been treated well?"

"Yes, I suppose so." She did not want to talk about the McIntyres, not now. It was too depressing, and she was too happy to see Philippe. "The people here are strange, different, and some of them hate Catholics so much. I don't know what I would have done without Leon. My Cousin Leon is on the Ramsey plantation, across the river."

"Yes, I know. That's how I found you. A man on a riverboat told me that there was a Frenchman named Leon Landry at the Ramsey plantation, so I went to see if he knew where you were. Leon sent me to the McIntyres, and their cook told me you were here."

"Did you see Mrs. McIntyre?"

"No, only the cook knows I'm here." He gave a short laugh. "When you're on the road, you always try to find the kitchen first."

"I still can't believe you're here. There were times when I thought I'd give my life just to hear your voice." Theresa sighed. "Philippe, is it my imagination, or were the people in Acadia better? Wasn't our life better than anything you've seen in the colonies?"

"Yes, the people were better, and life was happier." He stroked her slowly with the hands whose touch she remembered so well. "Perhaps I can find work in the area, now that I've found you."

"I think it would be better if we left," she replied, turning away.

"Why? It's hard enough for a Frenchman to get work anywhere. Do you think the McIntyres could use me?"

"I'm afraid to ask. I don't want to go back to the McIntyres. They'll prevent our marrying."

"Why? If they give me work or help me find something, there's no reason why you shouldn't stay with them until we can make better arrangements. You told me you weren't treated badly."

"I didn't tell you everything. I—I didn't want to upset you."

"What is it? Out with it."

"The truth is that Dr. McIntyre is, I mean, he has been— making advances to me."

Philippe's face burned a dark ugly red. "If he lays a hand on you, I'll murder him," he said. "He hasn't forced you, has he?"

"No, I've managed to avoid him. I didn't want to tell you, Philippe! I knew how angry you'd be! Do you think Leon can help us?"

"He said he couldn't get me work. I'm not sure why. Is Leon still after you?"

Theresa stood up and whirled around. "How did you know?"

"Everyone knew. I'm only surprised he waited so long. Has he asked you to marry him?"

"Yes, but of course I said no. Still, if I appeal to him, he might be able to do something for us."

"No! We've no option now but to leave. I've thought about going to Louisiana. It's the closest place that's owned by the French. But Theresa, it's a long, hard trip for a woman. The two of us will travel even more slowly than I can alone."

"I don't care. Let's risk it, Philippe."

He started buttoning her clothes slowly, but then he began kissing her again.

"I don't care. Anything at all will be better than going back to the McIntyres. We can survive anything if we're together." Theresa fell into her lover's arms.

Later, as they were dressing, Theresa was grateful for the fact that she had worn her cloak. At least she would have that much protection from the elements during their journey.

At the barnyard door, Philippe looked out at the setting sun, Theresa at his side. "It's settled. We're off to Louisiana."

Chapter Twelve

The days that followed were the happiest Theresa had ever known. With nothing but the clothes on their backs and Philippe's survival equipment—some gold coins, a musket, a horse, whose saddlebags contained flints for starting fires, blankets, ammunition, and a good supply of beef jerky—the two lovers struck out toward the south. When they came to Chesapeake Bay, they paid a boatman to carry them across and then headed in the direction of the French Catholic territory of Louisiana.

Theresa rode behind Philippe, as she had done during their aborted attempt to escape deportation on Grand Pré, and as long as her arms were around him and her head rested on the nape of his strong neck, she was blissfully happy. At night, they slept under the stars, making love beneath pine or maple or birch trees whose branches swayed gently in the cool April breeze. Afterward, they would fall asleep with their arms around each other. Their bed was made each evening from Philippe's blankets, placed on the ground and folded to make a warm cushion and to soften the hard earth, and Theresa was grateful that she had her own cloak to wrap about her. The nights were still cold, and there were times when Theresa would waken from the chill, only to find Philippe tenderly tucking her cloak about her. She'd lean back, content, tracing the contours of his face with gentle fingers.

Philippe's skill in hunting, fishing, and living in the wild put them in good stead. They avoided towns, fearing that their French accents would mark them as French aliens or that Dr. McIntyre had reported Theresa's running away and she would be recognized. Game and fish were plentiful, and Philippe shot deer and pheasant and other game or speared fish with a pointed stick while Theresa built a fire, which, under Philippe's guidance, she had learned to do by striking sparks from a flint. At nightfall, they would roast the day's catch over a slow fire, at peace with each other and the world.

At first, there was a great deal of conjecture about the McIntyres' reaction to Theresa's departure. "They'll question the slaves, and Dicey will have to tell Dr. McIntyre that she saw you and gave you directions to the farm," Theresa said. "There they'll find one naked goose and a half-filled bag of feathers!" She laughed. "Won't that old sourpuss be shocked! I can hear her now." She gave a wicked imitation of Mrs. McIntyre's high, screeching voice. " 'What did I tell you, Edmund! That little French hussy has taken off with a man! But what else could we expect from one like her? Blood will tell in the end!' "

They laughed, and Philippe drew her to him, kissing the tip of her nose. "Tell me again what you heard of my parents," Theresa asked. Philippe had already told her all he knew of them, but it was days before she tired of quizzing him, hoping each time that he would remember some particle of information he had forgotten previously.

"All I really know is that they were sent to Pennsylvania. I saw Daniel LeBlanc in Philadelphia, and he had heard that much of them. I didn't find them, however."

"Did the family manage to stay together? Did little Evariste and Richard survive the journey?"

"I don't know, pet. I didn't see them myself. I only know that they're living somewhere in Pennsylvania."

Both of Philippe's parents were now dead, and the rest of his family had been scattered. The younger children had gone with one of his sisters, Amalie, and although he had not been able to see them, he knew that they had been sent to Massachusetts. His other brothers and sisters had apparently been flung to the four winds. "You're my family now, Theresa," he would say, drawing her face to his shoulder and kissing the top of her head.

Occasionally, they would encounter another traveler on the rutted tracks through the forest that passed for roads. They would only nod in greeting and ride past in silence. More often, Philippe avoided the beaten path altogether. They had been gone for about a week when a stranger approached them, riding north. They had heard his horse coming, and Philippe was about to draw his horse aside, into the deep quiet of the woods, when he stopped suddenly.

"What is it, love?" Theresa asked, hugging him from behind.

"He's singing—listen!"

"So?" She shrugged. "Many a man sings to while away the monotonous hours of travel."

"Yes, but he's singing in Latin!"

Theresa strained to listen. She felt a mounting excitement as she realized that what Philippe had said was true—she could recognize the Latin words she had heard so often when Father Menard celebrated the mass in Grand Pré.

They peered cautiously ahead, and around the bend they saw a hawk-faced man, with graying hair, riding a roan stallion and wearing the flat-brimmed black hat and the black cassock of a Catholic priest. "My God! A Catholic priest!" Philippe whispered excitedly. "Theresa—he can marry us!"

"Are you sure it's safe to speak to him?" They had spoken to strangers as little as possible since their flight from the McIntyres' farm, and Theresa was hesitant to approach anyone.

"Yes, of course. He won't betray us." Philippe clicked his tongue and dug his heels gently into his horse's side, urging him back onto the path.

The priest approached them, singing softly in an off-key voice. "You speak to him, Theresa, in English," Philippe

93

whispered. His English was of the most rudimentary sort, and he puzzled over any sentences that were not the simplest.

"Please, Father, you are a Catholic priest, are you not?" Theresa inquired timidly as the man drew abreast of them.

"Why, yes, my child. Are you Catholic? Your accent is French." The harsh lines of the man's face softened, and when he smiled, he was almost handsome.

"Oh, yes, yes, we are, both of us. My name is Theresa Landry, and this is my fiancé, Philippe Bernard. We are refugees from Acadia."

The priest's face was suddenly sober. "Yes, we heard of the expulsion from Nova Scotia. A dreadful affair, truly dreadful—so much needless suffering. There are some of your people in Baltimore, in a community the English call Frenchtown, and a shipload of Acadians landed in Annapolis, too."

"You are English?" Theresa knew that there were some English Catholics in Maryland, but she had never met an English Catholic priest.

"Yes. My name is Father Boswell. I am going to minister to the English Catholics in Annapolis and to any other Catholics that may be there, of course. Where are you going? Have you no employment?"

"We were sent to Oxford but ran away. We were harshly treated there." Theresa was ashamed at how easily she lied, and to a priest, too, but she was afraid to tell him of Philippe's rebellious adventures. The man was, after all, an Englishman, and his sympathies might lie with his countrymen.

"And where are you going?"

"To Louisiana. Where else will Frenchmen be hospitably received?"

"It's a long trip, but you're probably right to go there. I hear that they welcome any Catholic settlers. It's a sparsely populated territory."

Theresa warmed to the sympathetic tone of his voice. "We were wondering, Father Boswell, if you might marry us," she asked shyly. "We intended to be married in Acadia, but we were deported before the banns were published. Then it was not possible in Oxford."

94

"I understand. And your young man, Philippe—can he speak for himself?"

"He speaks little English."

"That's all right. I speak French."

The three of them dismounted while Father Boswell conversed with Philippe, and having satisfied himself that both Theresa and Philippe were good Catholics and that there was no impediment to their marriage, he agreed to perform the ceremony. So it was that Theresa and Philippe became man and wife beneath the delicate spring green of a spreading cherry tree, with a bunch of snowy white apple blossoms in Theresa's hands for a bridal wreath.

"I'll buy you a ring as soon as I can," Philippe whispered as he kissed his bride.

"Oh, Philippe, I'm so happy," said Theresa, throwing her arms around him impulsively after the modest ceremony. She had thought to be married in the Church of St. Charles in Grand Pré, given away by her father in a proper bridal gown, but as she looked about at the beautiful spring leaves rustling in the breeze, she thought that only the presence of her family could have made her wedding a happier occasion.

They had nothing but beef jerky to eat, but this they offered to share with Father Boswell. He smiled and raised his hand. "No, keep your food. I've some of my own, and my flock will be expecting me in Annapolis. I'd best press on if I'm to arrive there on time. God bless you both, and good luck in Louisiana." With that, he departed, leaving Theresa and Philippe to spend their first afternoon and evening together as man and wife.

Two days later, Philippe's horse developed a bad limp, and Philippe was dismayed to discover that the joints of their mount's right foreleg were badly swollen. Up until that time, they had made good progress and were now in the colony of Virginia.

"If we continue riding, it will only get worse," he said after examining the horse's leg. "We'll have to find another mount."

"How are we going to get another horse out here in the woods?"

"We'll have to steal one."

"Steal? Become horse thieves? We'll be hanged if we're caught!" Theresa exclaimed.

"Then we'll have to see to it that we're not caught," he said grimly. "We'll have to shoot our horse, too, Theresa," he added. He held up his hand when she began to protest and read the look of consternation on her face. "I'm sorry, but he's only a liability now, and we can't leave him here to starve."

Theresa put her hands over her ears but could not shut out the sound of Philippe's musket firing. After Philippe had dispatched their horse, he and Theresa hid in the woods by the side of the road and watched for a rider. Travelers had become more frequent since they had entered Virginia, and they had not long to wait. A stout man on a sturdy bay, followed by a youth riding a roan stallion and leading another one that could have been its twin, came trotting by.

"I can't believe our luck," Philippe whispered. "They've got an extra horse."

"How are we going to get it?" Theresa whispered back.

"It's getting late. They'll have to stop for the night soon. We'll just follow them."

The man and boy were soon out of sight, but Theresa and Philippe followed them down the path on foot, slowed down even further by the gear that they carried with them. By the time they caught up with the pair, it was well after dark, and their victims reclined beside a small fire. They had already eaten and were settling in for the night, using their saddles as pillows.

Theresa and Philippe waited patiently in the woods until the steady breathing of the man and boy indicated that they were in a deep sleep. Then Philippe slipped soundlessly around the pair and approached their three horses, which were tethered a short distance away. Philippe had always shown great skill in handling animals, especially horses, and his rapport with beasts put him in good stead as he whispered softly to the one he selected. The animal twitched its ears and whinnied softly, allowing Philippe to scratch its muzzle and then, ever so gently, untie its reins and lead it very slowly, a

96

step at a time, away from its owners. The two other horses switched their tails and skipped a few nervous paces, while Theresa, her heart in her mouth, stood guard with Philippe's loaded muskets. Their two victims were obviously exhausted from traveling and snored quietly during the action.

When Philippe was a short distance away, Theresa joined him. While he loaded their new mount, she sat staring back in the direction of the men they had robbed. What had become of her? She thought of the simple, trusting girl she had been in Grand Pré. She had been as honest as the day was long, and now she was lying and deceitful, and a thief to boot. She looked back on the old days with longing, mourning her lost innocence, but she had had no choice but to change if she were to triumph over a treacherous, cruel world. She wanted to be simple again, but she felt that something had been smashed inside of her when her family had been deported. She had been broken, fragmented, and it had made her devious and conniving. It was as if she and Philippe were Adam and Eve after their expulsion from the garden of Eden, forced to struggle for survival in an alien world.

Philippe swung his saddlebags onto their new mount as Theresa sat musing over these gloomy thoughts. "Hurry," he said as he loaded their gear. "You've no time for regrets."

They traveled slowly on foot, leading their horse, and the next morning they skirted the stockade at Fredericksburg, which bristled with redcoats. Not far south of the town, they ran into a sortie of soldiers. When Philippe spotted them, he tried unsuccessfully to slip around them. "Halt!" one of them cried, his musket pointed at Philippe's chest. The other soldiers ran forward and grabbed their horse by the bridle.

"Get down!" they ordered. Philippe and Theresa obediently dismounted.

"Where are you going?"

"South," Theresa replied.

"You'd better come along with us," the party leader commanded, pushing Philippe in the back with his musket.

Inside the stockade, the commander, a Captain Brady, was summoned. A quick examination satisfied him that Theresa and Philippe were two alien French traveling south illegally.

"I'll have to hold you," he said. He looked at Theresa sharply. "There was an advertisement in the Maryland newspapers for a runaway French servant, a young woman who matched your description," he said. "She ran away in the company of a young Frenchman with red hair. Wait just a minute."

He disappeared into a building inside the stockade and returned with a newspaper. "Were you employed by a Dr. McIntyre?" he asked Theresa.

"Please, sir, my husband and I mean no one any harm. We only want to be allowed to go on our way in peace."

"Answer my question," Captain Brady said roughly. "Were you employed by a Dr. McIntyre?"

Theresa sensed that further opposition was futile. "Yes, sir," she answered.

"Then you'll be returned to him. As for you, young man, I'll decide what to do with you later."

"Please don't send me back," Theresa pleaded, fixing her large dark eyes on Captain Brady. "Philippe and I have been married, properly, by a priest."

"A likely story," said Captain Brady. "And where would you find a papist priest in the woods?"

"But we did," she retorted desperately as she was dragged off. "He was a Father Boswell, on his way to the Catholics in Annapolis."

But she had already been dismissed. Captain Brady had turned her over to one of his men, with the orders that she was to be returned by ship with a party of soldiers going north. "You may collect the reward and get this Dr. McIntyre to pay for her return passage."

"Good-bye, Philippe. I love you," she cried out in French.

Philippe yelled back, "Theresa, I'll come for you again, never fear! I love you!"

Theresa was grasped roughly by the arm and walked to a dock by the edge of the Potomac River where a full-rigged ship lay rocking gently in her moorings. She spent a miserable night lying on the open deck. The next day, the ship made its way south, down the Potomac River, until it entered Chesapeake Bay; then it turned north. Theresa was so miserable and so sick with worry over Philippe's fate that she did not even count the days she traveled. When they reached the mouth of the Choptank River, she and the soldier were transferred to a small boat, and by the time evening arrived, they were in Oxford, at the threshold of Dr. McIntyre's house.

Moses answered the soldier's knock. His usually impassive expression turned to one of sorrow when he spotted Theresa. "I'm sorry they caught you," he whispered under his breath while the soldier negotiated with Dr. McIntyre for the reward. "We all prayed you and your man would get away."

It was Wednesday evening, and Mrs. McIntyre was at prayer meeting, so Theresa had only to face the interrogation of the doctor. "I thought we had reached an understanding, Theresa," he said in his most self-pitying voice. "I'm sorry to find you so deceitful."

Theresa choked back her dislike of the man and forced herself to answer him civilly. "My fiancé came for me from Acadia," she replied.

"You could have trusted me. I would have found him some employment if he had come to me."

Theresa doubted the truth of this pronouncement, but she held her tongue. She was suddenly fatigued, so tired that she could hardly stand. "You may go to bed and resume your duties tomorrow," the doctor said, dismissing her.

The next day, Theresa returned to her work in the dispensary as if nothing had happened. She now had the additional burden of helping Pammy tend her herb garden, and she was sent into the woods to collect the healing plants that grew wild.

The slaves all regretted that she had not gotten away. "I'm sorry I told the McIntyres about your young man," said Dicey, "but what could I do? They asked us all over and over again what we knew. I was afraid they'd find out he had been here some other way, and then the fat would have been in the fire. I didn't know who else had seen him. I knew your cousin, Leon Landry, from the Ramsey plantation saw him."

"That's all right, Dicey. I don't blame you." It was the same old tale—helplessness on the part of slaves and servants in the face of a power structure they had no part in.

Theresa returned to her weary round of duties in the dispensary and in the cold, unhappy McIntyre house. Life proceeded as it had before her brief escape with Philippe, until a day in the middle of the summer when she could no longer conceal from herself the fact that she was going to bear a child.

Chapter Thirteen

When Theresa realized that she was pregnant, her first thought was to confide in Pammy, who was, after all, the person next to Dr. McIntyre most experienced in such matters. She waited for a few days, trying to think of a way to broach the subject. Pammy was not a person in whom one confided easily. Theresa had at first assumed that she and Pammy would become friends since they worked so closely together, but Pammy remained aloof. Behind her placid exterior, Theresa sensed a profound anger. The other slaves she knew seemed to accept their condition with a certain resignation, and some were quite proud of their status as house, as opposed to yard or field, slaves. Even Moses, who had a low opinion of Dr. and Mrs. McIntyre and took a sly pleasure in "getting over," or deceiving, his masters, seemed to regard them with some affection. Theresa suspected that Pammy hated all white people, even Theresa, who was almost as powerless as the slaves.

At last, Pammy gave Theresa her opening. "You been awful quiet lately," she remarked one day.

"I'm going to have a baby," Theresa blurted out.

A slow smile curled Pammy's lip. "So that's it."

"You don't seem to be surprised."

Pammy shrugged. "It don't make me no never mind.

Massa the father?'' She said it so casually that Theresa was stung.

"No, why do you think that?"

"Don't tell me he ain't tried you yet."

Theresa had told no one of what had transpired between Dr. McIntyre and her, but she told Pammy now. "You handled him pretty good. You sure he ain't the father?"

"Yes, I'm sure."

"You sure are lucky. We all figured it was just a question of time."

"But I've been here for a long time."

"So? He don't amuse himself with the help until his fine ladies run out on him. Georgeanna Caffery and old Cecilia Hathaway both dropped Massa a while back. That's why the old fool been drinking so much lately. He figure he losing his touch. It ain't so easy to charm the ladies now that he's got gray hair and a fat belly." Then, letting down her guard at last, she said, "He didn't get after me until Rosalie Dodson dumped him."

"Dr. McIntyre has forced his attentions upon you?"

"Child, where you been? Why you think my son Willie got such light skin?"

"Oh," Theresa said blankly. "I never thought about it."

"I had a man—a fine man, too. Massa sold him across the river to the Ramseys to break us up. My Ned took up with another woman, and they got a family now. And me? I got Massa's bastard. That old hag treat me like dirt because she know. As if I had anything to say about it, as if I wanted him. She had me beaten for nothing. She treat me so bad even Massa get ashamed. He give me this job to make up for it."

"Wasn't there anything you could do?"

"Do what? I'm just a piece of meat as far as they concerned."

She spoke with such bitterness that Theresa felt the flesh rise on her arms, and had to look away. "I guess you must hate them."

"You don't know nothing about hate. I'd murder them in their clean white bed if I thought I could get away with it." The words came out in a rush. Then she gave Theresa a sharp look, and her face closed again. "But that's another story.

102

We got you to worry about now. Is the father that man you run away with?''

"Yes. He's my husband. We were married."

"That won't help you much if he ain't here. Don't worry—I'll get rid of it for you."

"Get rid of it? But I can't do that." I could never kill Philippe's child, Theresa thought.

"You can't afford to think that way. Do you know what they do to white servants who have children their masters don't want? If that old bitch don't toss you out in the street, she have you lashed for sure."

"Lashed?"

"Twenty lashes for bastardy. That about the only advantage to being a slave. If a slave have a baby, everybody happy, 'cause that make another slave. If a servant have a baby, that another mouth to feed, and it slows the mother down with her work. Twenty lashes, that what the law give you if Missus take you to court. I seen a white girl get lashed once. They stripped her to the waist in the town square, and every old lecher in town gather round to drool. After the eighth stroke, she passed out, but they kept on going, anyway."

"My baby won't be a bastard. Philippe and I are married. Besides, I don't care what happens to me. I'm going to keep my baby." Theresa's first thought when she realized she was going to have a child was that at least she would not be alone anymore. Besides, Philippe might return any day. She had to cling to that hope—she could not believe that he would be defeated by the English.

"Who says they let you keep it? If they let you stay, I bet they bind the baby out."

"Bind it out?"

Pammy sighed. "Lord, you don't know nothing. If a servant is indentured, that means his employer pays for his ship passage and he has to work for seven years. If a child is too young to do work, he gets bound out. That means whoever takes him supports him when he's little; then he has to work many years to pay for his keep. If Massa and Missus don't want your child, they take it away from you and bind it out to somebody."

"Surely they can't do that. Surely they can't take my baby away from me."

"Surely they can, if they want to. You ain't got any say in the matter. Will the father come for you?"

"If he can. He was captured by soldiers and held in a stockade."

Pammy shook her head and sighed audibly. "Honey, you sure got yourself in a heap of trouble. You think it over, and let me know if you want me to get rid of it. But don't wait too long. The longer you wait, the more dangerous it is."

Theresa knew she would have her child but thanked Pammy for her advice. One good thing seemed to have come of the mess she was in—the ice between the two women was broken.

After her conversation with Pammy, Theresa lay awake at night worrying about how she was to keep her baby. If only Philippe would return! She decided at last that anything was better than her constant agonizing. It would be better to have it out with the McIntyres right away and get their response. She would tell them herself before the baby became obvious.

Before she had summoned her nerve to confront her employers, she received a visit from Leon. They found themselves alone together in the kitchen, and in the middle of his recital about his latest successes at the Ramsey plantation, she interrupted him.

"Leon, I'm going to have a baby."

He stopped in midsentence. "You are what?"

"I'm going to have a baby."

"Philippe's?" he asked, his face flushed.

"Yes."

"Oh, no." He wore a look of such distress that she could not go on. "Are you sure?"

"Yes. It's all right, Leon. We were married by a priest on his way to Annapolis. I'm sure Philippe will return to me."

Leon took a deep breath and gave Theresa a troubled look. "Theresa, I wish you'd told me about the marriage earlier. I've heard some bad news, and I didn't know how to break it to you. You know how news travels up and down the river."

She did, indeed. Next to newspapers, which many of the colonists could not read, the greatest source of information was news carried by travelers on land or water. "I heard from

104

a riverboat captain that there was an execution of a Frenchman in Virginia. He was a man with red hair."

Theresa sank slowly to the bench in the kitchen, her face suddenly white and drawn. "When did you hear that? Why didn't you tell me at once?"

"I just heard. I didn't know how to tell you."

"Was it because of that cursed horse?"

"What horse?"

"Philippe's horse went lame, and we had to steal another."

"It could well have been. The theft of a horse is a capital offense. Don't make any decision yet, Theresa. Before you talk to the McIntyres, let me think for a while."

"All right," she said dully. Nothing mattered now if what Leon had told her was true. Still, riverboat information was often unreliable. Somehow she could not believe Philippe was dead.

As distressed as he was by the news that she and Philippe had been married, an even more troubling thought passed through Leon's mind. "At home—were you, did you—"

"Yes. Philippe and I became lovers after my father told us we couldn't marry."

"You were willing to ignore your father's wishes?"

"I loved Philippe. I still do."

Leon tried to size up the situation. "Who else knows?"

"I've told Pammy. She told me she could get rid of the baby, but I won't hear of it."

"Don't do anything until I have time to think this over. I'll come back to see you next Sunday."

Leon spent the next week in a torment as great as Theresa's own. Night after night he tortured himself with the picture of Theresa and Philippe in each other's arms. As painful as the thought was, he found that it also aroused him. He saw Theresa as a wanton woman, laughing seductively as she held out her arms to Philippe, and the thought made him grow hard with desire. Bitch, strumpet—not the pure maiden he had thought her to be but equally as desirable. He groaned with longing as he found his own release between the sheets of his bed. He imagined Theresa as a painted whore, dressed in beads and a dress of gaudy silk cut so low it uncovered the tops of her swelling breasts. He saw her offering herself to a succession of strangers for money, smiling and whispering insincere words of love, secretly despising them all for the fools that they were. His Theresa, his love. . . .

He thought at first that there could be no further question of marriage between them. She had been defiled and could never truly belong to him. As the week progressed, he was bewildered by the fact that his interest in her had not abated at all—if anything, it had been inflamed by her revelation. He did not understand this until it occurred to him that in addition to the advantages supplied by his sex and education, he now had the advantage of being able to save her child for her. The McIntyres would probably not believe that she and Philippe had been married—the coincidence that they had run into a Catholic priest in the woods during their brief flight was too great. Even if it were true, she would not be believed. Why hadn't she mentioned it earlier if she were a married woman? She would be treated like a fallen woman, but he could lift her again and make her respectable. He would raise another man's child as his own, something not many men would be willing to do. He, Leon, would still condescend to marry Theresa, miserable creature that she was. He would be noble; he would be magnanimous—and he would also have a weapon to hold over her head should he ever need it. Should she ever balk at his commands, he would only need to remind her of the disgrace from which he had saved her.

It bothered him that he had lied to Theresa about hearing news of Philippe's death, but after her revelation about the theft of the horse, it was a pretty good guess that Philippe was dead. If the theft had been discovered, it was almost a certainty. It would be difficult for Philippe to work his way back to Oxford even if he were alive. Surely Leon could be forgiven stretching the truth a bit. He loved Theresa so much, and she would be so much better off with him. His fortunes were rising steadily on the Ramsey plantation, and the fields he had been given to experiment with crop rotation were flourishing.

It was with the utmost pride in his virtue and rectitude that he informed Theresa, on the following Sunday, that he was prepared to make an honest woman of her.

106

"I'm sorry, Leon," she replied without a moment's hesitation. "I can't marry you. But thank you for the offer."

Leon was stunned. It had never even occurred to him that he would be refused under the present circumstances. "You can't be serious. Do you realize the position you're in? You can't bear this child alone. The McIntyres will put you out in the street. You never told them that you were married. They'll think you're lying if you tell them so now."

"I'm willing to take my chances. Besides, somehow I can't believe that Philippe is dead."

"Surely you're not foolish enough to pin your hopes on Philippe?" Leon was livid. "Hasn't he proven himself irresponsible enough already? He should have waited to—to marry you until you arrived in Louisiana and he was able to give you a home. How do you know this man you met was a priest? He could have been an impostor." Leon floundered on in desperation. "You don't even know that the marriage was legal."

"Philippe isn't like that. If he's alive, he'll come for me. I know he will."

"Think of your child's future if you won't think of your own. I've been doing very well for myself, Theresa. My experiment with crop rotation seems to be a success, and the entire Ramsey family is taking note of me. They are also becoming aware of what Caleb Wheeler is costing them, and I have a feeling his days are numbered." Leon looked around the kitchen to reassure himself that they were entirely alone and lowered his voice. "Really, my dear, I should not take the liberty of divulging this information, and perhaps such an announcement is premature, but Nathaniel Ramsey has led me to understand—I mean, I have been given to hope that in the event of Wheeler's dismissal . . ." Leon raised his eyebrows suggestively and let his voice trail off, waiting for Theresa to finish his sentence.

"Yes—you have reason to hope what?" Theresa asked with a note of impatience.

"I have reason to believe that one day the Ramseys may do me the honor of making me their overseer."

Theresa looked at the expression of self-satisfaction on her cousin's face and decided that Leon was unquestionably the most pompous creature she had ever met. "That's very nice, Leon," she said without enthusiasm.

"Nice? Is that all you can say—nice? Do you realize what an honor it would be for me, and for you, as my wife? Do you realize how hard I've had to work, what kind of prejudice I've had to overcome as a foreigner from Acadia?"

"Yes, I know, and I'm very proud of you."

"But you won't marry me."

"No."

Leon lost his temper at last. "Are you mad? Have you no pride, no consideration for your family name? Are you willing to disgrace us all?" Leon's anger evaporated as quickly as it had come. He turned to Theresa with a look of pleading. "What do you want, Theresa? What is it you want that I haven't got?"

Theresa answered him slowly, considering. She had never put it into words herself. "I want to enjoy my life. I want to wait for Philippe and raise our children, and I want to have fun doing it. I'm only seventeen years old. I want to feel young. I want to laugh again. I want to go to a dance. I'm willing to work hard, as hard as I can, but I want to have a good time, too. Otherwise, what is life all about? When they nail the lid on my coffin, what difference will anything else make if I haven't enjoyed myself?"

"And you can't enjoy yourself with me." Leon rose to leave. "Then you're a fool. I won't renew my offer, and you'll not get another one like it. I don't intend to visit you again."

"I'm sorry, Leon. I hope you'll get over your anger and come back to see me. I do treasure our friendship. Your company has meant a lot to me."

"Not enough, apparently. Good-bye—I'll not trouble you again."

Theresa delayed her talk with the McIntyres as long as she could on the slim chance that Philippe might suddenly appear and save her. By the first of August, she was having to suck in her breath to fasten her dress, and she had to make a conscious effort throughout the day to hold her stomach in as far as she could. Pammy looked at her waistline as she went about her daily tasks and shook her head.

108

One night, the McIntyres retired to the parlor after the evening meal and sat together, talking amiably, in a rare mood of relaxation. Theresa knew she could wait no longer. She knocked on the door and entered, her heart thudding.

The McIntyres looked up. "Yes, Theresa, what is it?" her mistress asked sharply.

"I must talk to you both. I'm—I'm going to have a baby," she whispered.

A dead silence followed her announcement. Mrs. McIntyre spoke at last. "I can't believe it, after all my attempts to educate you, to see to your spiritual welfare! After my husband and I took you right off the boat, filthy, with nothing but a few rags on your back. I told you she was foreign trash and would come to no good," she said, wagging her finger at her husband. "I warned you against her. And look how she has repaid our kindness! A French papist! An instrument of the devil!" She paused, running out of invectives at last.

"But Philippe and I were married!"

"I don't believe you."

"It's true."

Dr. McIntyre, who had maintained his silence until this moment, spoke at last. "Don't badger her, Elizabeth. She feels bad enough as it is. The girl's far from home; she was lonely. She's only human. It could have happened to anybody."

"Oh, how noble of you to excuse her conduct! How do I know the child's not yours?"

Theresa drew in her breath. There had been no acknowledgement on Mrs. McIntyre's part that she was aware of her husband's nocturnal visits to Theresa's room.

"It's not his! It's Philippe's!" Theresa repeated stubbornly.

"And what do you plan to do? Surely you don't expect us to keep you?"

"I don't know. I wasn't sure." Theresa stammered.

"Stop that, Elizabeth. The girl's got nowhere to go. We can't kick her out into the street, baby or no baby."

"I won't have her under my roof! I won't have her disgracing our household! I'm a good Christian! I'm a good Christian woman!" shrieked Mrs. McIntyre, her face twisted with malice.

"For once you'll do as I say, and I say she'll not be put

out," her husband said sharply. Mrs. McIntyre winced at her husband's tone of command.

"And do you expect me to let her walk around here, heavy-bellied, for everyone to laugh at?"

"We'll send her to the farm until the baby's born. Then she can resume her duties here."

"I don't like it. I don't like it at all."

"I didn't ask you whether you liked it or not. That's the way it's going to be," the doctor ordered.

"Very well, but I want her out of my sight by tomorrow morning. I'll not lay eyes on her again until this disgraceful affair is concluded."

Later, in bed, Theresa felt too dazed by her good fortune to sleep. Dr. McIntyre would take care of her. He would not let her be beaten in the square or thrown out into the street. She could have embraced him from sheer relief.

The next morning, at breakfast, Theresa told the slaves in the kitchen that she was going to the farm—and the reason why. Everyone took the news calmly and agreed that she was fortunate to have received Dr. McIntyre's protection. After breakfast, Dicey took her aside. "Is it that Frenchman that come through here last April?"

"Yes."

"I thought so. The timing was right."

"Dicey, Leon heard that Philippe was dead, but I just can't believe it's true! We were married when I ran away; truly we were. If Philippe comes back while I'm away, tell him where I am," she begged.

"I will. Does your cousin still want to marry you?" The slaves had watched Leon's courtship of Theresa with interest.

"Yes, but I can't."

"I know you don't tingle when he look at you, but sometimes you got to be practical."

"I know, but I'm not going to be that practical unless I'm really desperate."

Dicey laughed until her huge breasts swayed. "He sure stuck on himself, that Leon!"

The following January, Theresa was delivered of a baby boy whom she named Gaspard for her father. When little

Gaspard was three months old, she returned to the McIntyre house. The doctor checked him and pronounced him to be healthy, but Mrs. McIntyre refused to look at the infant or acknowledge his existence in any way.

Gaspard slept with Theresa in her attic room at night, and she took him with her to the dispensary during the day. From the moment Theresa looked into her baby's round blue eyes, her life changed forever. She would never be alone again. He was hers, her very own baby, and she loved him as fiercely as she loved Philippe. She still waited, hoping daily for Philippe's return, but more than a year after his visit, she had still not heard a word from him. In the back of her mind, a nagging fear began growing that perhaps he was indeed dead.

That autumn, when Gaspard was nine months old, he suffered from an attack of croup that made him cough and cry incessantly for days. Theresa held him to her bosom at night, rocking him and trying to stifle his cries, afraid that he would keep the McIntyres awake. On the fourth night of his illness, Theresa had fallen into a fitful and exhausted sleep, so weary that she slept through the baby's wailing. She was awakened in the middle of the night by the voice of Mrs. McIntyre.

"Poor Robert! Don't cry; Mummy's coming," she muttered, bending over Theresa's bed.

Theresa, alarmed, looked at Mrs. McIntyre and picked up her son. Her mistress looked like a frightful apparition in the light of her candle, with wild eyes, sleep-swollen face, and a long gray braid hanging down from her nightcap.

"Don't cry, Robert. Everything will be all right. Mummy's here," she said, plucking the infant from Theresa's arms. Gaspard, frightened by the strange woman, let out a loud wail.

"Sh, sh," crooned Mrs. McIntyre, rocking him and clutching the infant to her bony bosom. The baby tightened his fists, screwed up his face, and screamed at the top of his lungs.

Mrs. McIntyre's eyes fell upon Theresa and widened as if she had only just noticed her. "What are you doing here?" she hissed over the baby's screams. "Jezebel, hussy, devil's spawn." Theresa held out her arms for her child. Mrs. McIntyre stepped back, pulling Gaspard from her reach. "Don't you touch him, you French whore."

"I'm sorry he woke you," said Theresa. "I tried to keep him quiet, but he has the croup."

"No, he has diphtheria. Robert has diphtheria. He'll stop crying if we can only get a wee bit of water down his throat."

"Mrs. McIntyre, that's my baby, Gaspard, and he has the croup." Mrs. McIntyre looked at Gaspard and dropped him as if he were hot. Theresa was barely able to catch him before he hit the floor.

"Bastard," spat Mrs. McIntyre. "Filthy French bastard. Not my Robert." She bent over the bed and slapped Gaspard's face.

Without thinking, Theresa drew back her hand and struck Mrs. McIntyre as hard as she could. "How dare you! How dare you strike a sick child!" she raged over Gaspard's screams.

Mrs. McIntyre staggered back, her mouth round with surprise. "You—you insolent—"

"I'm sorry," said Theresa, trembling with fear. "I'm so tired. My baby is so ill. . . ."

"Your baby, your baby," Mrs. McIntyre sneered. "Comfort him while you may. He'll be gone soon enough."

"What do you mean?" Theresa asked, drawing the child to her.

"I mean I've made arrangements to bind him out to the Latimers as soon as he's weaned," she answered, relishing the panic in Theresa's eyes.

"You can't mean it," she replied in a whisper. "The doctor won't allow it."

"He will, and he has," Mrs. McIntyre answered with triumph. "It was the bargain we struck. I agreed to keep you if he'd let me dispose of the baby. He hadn't the stomach to tell you himself, weakling that he is. Surely you didn't expect me to keep my husband's bastard under my roof?"

"Oh, no," said Theresa. "Please, Mrs. McIntyre, I beg you to let me keep my baby. Gaspard's not your husband's, I promise."

"How do you expect me to believe a word you say? Even if you were married to your elusive Frenchman, you were carrying on with my husband before you ran away. I know you were, you little strumpet.'' Mrs. McIntyre turned on her heel and slammed the door behind her.

Despite Theresa's weariness, she could not sleep another wink. She lay trying to quiet her baby and think at the same time. She could no longer delude herself that Philippe was alive. Surely he could have come for her by now! She was going to lose her Gaspard if she did not act at once.

Only a week before, she had learned that Leon had indeed been made the overseer of the Ramsey plantation. It was a great responsibility to place in the hands of a Frenchman who had been in their employ not quite two years, but Caleb Wheeler had at last been dismissed, and another harvest season was imminent. Theresa saw her only hope.

When the first light of dawn streaked the sky, she arose, wrapped Gaspard in a blanket, and slipped down the stairs as quietly as she could. Out into the gray light she stumbled. When the ferryman arrived to make his first run across the river, she was ready, with a linen handkerchief to pay her fare. She and Gaspard were the only passengers. A fine mist swirled up from the water as the ferryman poled them silently across. He asked no questions, and they did not exchange a word.

On the other side, she shifted the baby to her other arm and staggered down the road to the small whitewashed house Leon had been given when the Ramseys made him their overseer. She was so exhausted that spots danced before her eyes.

Leon was just finishing breakfast when she arrived at his door. ''Theresa!'' he said. ''What are you doing here?''

''I have come to marry you, Leon.''

In the next room, she placed Gaspard in Leon's bed and was asleep herself almost before her head touched the pillow.

Leon sat by his bed, watching Theresa sleep, a powerful emotion of triumph swelling inside him. His patience was going to be rewarded—at last, Theresa would be his. He

113

smiled down at the sleeping girl and pushed a few moist curls off her forehead. She looked like a small child as she slept, her mouth open, her long eyelashes curled on her cheek. His Theresa, whom he had loved so long, within his reach at last. . . .

When Theresa awoke, she told Leon what had transpired at the McIntyres' the night before, and he told her calmly that he had sent for the Anglican minister from Oxford. They could be married as soon as he arrived.

"Oh, no, Leon, we must be married by a Catholic priest," she protested. "We won't truly be married unless we're married by a real priest."

"But there is no Catholic priest in Oxford. We'll have to send for the nearest one, and it could take days for him to get here!"

"A few days won't make any difference now that we're here, now that we're safe." She reached for Gaspard, whose infection was clearing. He was getting the first good sleep he had had for days.

"I can't wait," said Leon, grabbing her playfully. "I'm an impatient bridegroom. We can be married later by a Catholic priest."

Theresa was too tired to argue any longer. "Let's discuss it later, Leon," she said meekly.

The Anglican priest arrived at dusk. Leon reasoned with Theresa for hours, but she was adamant. She would be married in a Roman Catholic ceremony or not at all. Finally, in desperation, Leon implored the Ramseys to send for the nearest Roman priest at once. They complied, amused at his haste, and gave Theresa a small guest room in their mansion until the priest arrived four days later.

The Ramseys proved to be generous people. When Theresa awoke at dawn, suddenly fearful of retaliation by the McIntyres, they offered to write a letter explaining the situation. The Ramseys would take full responsibility for the rearing of little Gaspard—and provide Theresa with a home. Elizabeth McIntyre, for her part, received the letter and breathed a sigh of relief. At last, that little hussy and her bastard will be out of my life forever, she thought.

Once Theresa recovered from her panic, she moved through

114

the days before her wedding in a dream, trying to resign herself to a lifetime spent with Leon. He was not a bad man, and one could not always have things as one wanted them. Perhaps growing up, becoming an adult, lay precisely in accepting that life was not perfect and making the best of things as they were. She had Gaspard, and Leon had an excellent position. . . . she tried not to rail against fate. If the Acadians had not been expelled from their homes, she and Philippe would be happily married by now. There was nothing she could do about that now, but Philippe would remain her great love until the end of her life. Nothing could take away the memories that she had of him. In her heart, she would always belong to him.

The Ramseys' nineteen-year-old daughter, Letitia, gave Theresa one of her own dresses to be married in. When the priest arrived at last, the Ramseys, glad of any excuse for a party, had gathered in the family chapel.

Theresa walked down the aisle in her new dress on the arm of the senior Mr. Ramsey, who had agreed to give her away, and looked dully at the smiling faces. Before the altar stood the priest and Leon, beaming with happiness and pride. You won, Leon, she thought. Your persistence won the day. It seemed to her that she was observing her own wedding from a great distance. She stood observing details of the chapel— the stained-glass window from which multicolored light poured, the beautiful lace altar cloth—as the priest moved through the service.

She still expected some reprieve. Surely Philippe would came stalking in at the last moment, striding down the aisle with his jaunty swagger, to claim her for his own. She even turned around once in the middle of the ceremony to look for him. But there was no miracle. She walked out into the bright September sunshine on Leon's arm, united in holy wedlock to a man she did not love.

Chapter Fourteen

The life Theresa moved into was not a bad one. She and Leon were not, of course, included in the Ramseys' social life, but they were treated with kindness and consideration, and they were even given the use of a slave to help Theresa with her housework and in the running of the dispensary she set up for the care of the Ramseys' slaves. Leon was for the most part good to her, although he was stiff and dictatorial. Yet Theresa could not overcome her initial distaste of sleeping with him. He was shy and fumbling in his approach to her, and he never took long. After a while, it merely became one of the things she did, like doing the wash or preparing her herb remedies. Still, she could not reconcile herself to bearing his children, and she used Pammy's method of preventing conception, which she found to be quite effective.

The only joy in her life was little Gaspard, who, it seemed to her, looked more and more like his grandfather every day. Even before he could talk, she began telling him stories of the wonderful man for whom he had been named and of her old life in Grand Pré. The child regarded her solemnly when she told him of such things, until she laughed at herself for talking to him of matters he could not possibly understand.

She thought of her father's doing the same thing to her when she had been small.

A year passed, marred only by Leon's constant disapproval of Theresa's failure to bear him a child. But in October a virulent epidemic of smallpox swept through Maryland. Theresa had heard that the disease had broken out in other parts of the colony, and she prayed that Talbot County might be spared. The first case Theresa nursed at her dispensary was the small daughter of one of the Ramseys' slaves. When the dreaded high fever and facial pustules left no doubt that smallpox had struck close to home, she took the ferry across the Choptank for a hurried consultation with Dr. McIntyre, who was always cordial, but aloof, since her marriage.

"No, I'm sorry," he answered in reply to her question. "There's not a single effective remedy that I know of beyond the application of cool damp rags to reduce the fever. A doctor in England has tried an interesting experiment, however. He noticed that people who have had smallpox once never get it again, so he came up with an ingenious theory. If you give a person a mild case of it by injecting fluid from smallpox sores, he will recover from that bout and not contract it a second time. Needless to say, no one was leaping with eagerness to test his theory! He tried it on some convicts who escaped the gallows by volunteering for the experiment, and sure enough, all of them had mild cases and survived. Still, no one else would try the remedy, so he injected his own son."

"Did the boy live?" Theresa asked anxiously. She was concerned for the safety of all those under her care, but most particularly, of course, for the welfare of her own son.

"Yes, he did, but I'm not brave enough to try it on myself or to urge it on my patients, and I would recommend the same course to you."

"Don't worry. Thank you, doctor." Theresa replied. She could hardly imagine herself injecting little Gaspard with the deadly poison. She returned home, lost in thought. Such miraculous discoveries medical science was making about the human body! There was always more to learn, and Theresa was a willing pupil. Dr. McIntyre had shown her how to facilitate difficult births, and Theresa was now called upon

117

for almost all the lyings-in on the plantation. She enjoyed healing the sick, and she knew she could turn to the doctor whenever an unusual or difficult case turned up. The doctor was pleased that Theresa took such an avid interest in medicine and helped her along—as long as she stayed out of his wife's way when she visited his home.

The very evening of her visit to Dr. McIntyre, little Gaspard fretted and whined over his supper, and when Theresa touched his forehead, she discovered that it was blazing hot. She put him to bed at once and sat up beside him half the night, keeping cool cloths on his head and praying that he had not contracted smallpox. Her worst fears were realized when the pus-filled bumps—which were the mark of the disease—appeared on his face the next day.

Leon did what he could to help her, but with the crops coming in, it was his busiest time, and he was fully occupied on the plantation. During the day, two more cases broke out among the slaves, and Theresa heard reports that several cases had been diagnosed among the citizens of Oxford. There was no question now that the epidemic, which was sweeping the colony, would not spare their little corner. Theresa sat by helplessly while the number of cases mounted. She cut down on her regular duties so that she could devote more attention to Gaspard, and she moved his bed into the dispensary's back room where she might watch him. After a week of working all day and sitting up with her sick child at night, she was so exhausted that she could hardly hold her head up.

The little boy put up a valiant fight for his life, but the smallpox proved too much for him. Theresa sat by with tears of weakness and misery coursing down her face as her firstborn, whom she loved so dearly and for whom she had sacrificed so much, relinquished his tenuous hold on life.

Gaspard died in the hour before dawn. Theresa, dazed and inconsolable, wandered down to the river's edge. She was haunted by memories of the child's labored breathing and the way his small fingers, burning with fever, had reached up to touch her cheek shortly before he died. She sat by the water's edge, staring at it without seeing; in disjointed sequence, the important events of her life passed before her eyes. Idle memories of her childhood rose to the surface and then of Philippe's courting her, culminating in her father's refusal to let them marry and their clandestine, defiant meetings in the Landrys' barn. She thought of the sorrow in her father's voice when he had told her the story of his first marriage and her own insistence that life with Philippe would not be like that.

"Wait a year," he had said to her. "If you still want to marry Philippe next harvest season, I'll let you." What blind optimism they had all felt about the future! Here it was three harvests later—a lifetime later, it seemed to Theresa—and she had been cruelly torn from her home and family, sent to a foreign land and into servitude, and had been wife to two men. One of them, the only one she really loved, had given her a child, and now, before his second birthday, she was to lay him in his grave. What had she to live for now? What was to prevent her from throwing herself into the river?

She looked at the churning, muddied waters of the Choptank and then looked up, idly, at a riverboat that was moving slowly up to the pier. "Here's where you wanted to get off," a man on board said. A man leaped nimbly ashore, and Theresa gazed incredulously at the slender form crowned with burnished red hair. It wasn't; it couldn't be—

"Philippe," she whispered. "Philippe." She sat staring at him, as if in a trance, tears running down her face, until he spotted her and came toward her, his arms outstretched. She did not move; it seemed to her that her limbs had turned to lead.

"Haven't you a kiss for your long-lost husband?" Philippe said with a laugh, falling to his knees before her and pulling her to him.

"Philippe," she said again, folding him in her arms and burying her face in his neck. She savored his warm, clean scent and then kissed him passionately, clinging to him for dear life. He's all I have left, she thought.

"They told me you were dead," she said as soon as she could speak. "Where have you been? I gave up hope. I couldn't wait any longer!" She was nearly incoherent, torn between excitement and sorrow.

"I almost did die. It took all my gold to bribe my way out of hanging over that pesky horse, and then I was put to work

119

on a tobacco plantation in Virginia. But I fled for the second time, was caught, and was sent south to Georgia to work on a cotton plantation. I might as well have been sent to hell! I was treated worse than a slave there!''

"Oh, Philippe, how did they catch you? You were so clever at avoiding the English soldiers in Acadia.''

"Yes, but I knew the country there, and I had the Indians to help me. Besides, the colonists down here hate the French so. It's a miracle I got here at all.''

"A miracle,'' she repeated. She recalled that it was a miracle she had prayed for, for days, while Gaspard lay fighting for his life. It was a prayer that had not been answered. Her shoulders slumped, and she buried her face in her hands.

"What is it, love?'' Philippe asked gently, trying to take her hands from her face. "I thought that you were happy to see me,'' he said with a touch of the old playful mockery. To his utter surprise, Theresa buried her face in his lap and began sobbing. She had not cried before, but now, with Philippe's comforting arms around her, the dam burst, and her grief poured out in a flood.

"He's dead,'' she managed to choke out between her sobs.

"Who's dead?''

"Our son, Gaspard.''

"We . . . a son?'' Philippe asked, stroking her head.

"Oh, yes, he was the dearest child that ever lived,'' Theresa said when she had gotten herself under control once more. "The most beautiful baby, with the best nature in the world. Now he's gone, and you never even got to see him, to know him.''

"Perhaps it's just as well if I had to lose him.''

"Yes,'' said Theresa, wiping her face and sitting up straight. She was determined to be brave, to put the past behind her. "There must be a reason for all this. Just when I thought I had nothing to live for, you arrived.''

Philippe took Theresa's hands in his own and brought them slowly to his lips. "Yes, truly, God works in mysterious ways.''

120

Chapter Fifteen

"Philippe! Catch Jacqueline!" Theresa Bernard clutched her box of herb cuttings and tried at the same time to supervise the loading of her possessions and small family onto the ship *Virgin*, bound for the Spanish territory of Louisiana. Her daughter, Jacqueline, who was nearly three, had broken loose and was running away from the wharf as fast as her chubby legs would carry her. Philippe dutifully eased the chest he was carrying from his shoulder and ran after the small girl.

Louisiana, recently transferred from France to Spain, had issued an invitation to all the Acadians still living in the English colonies to settle the sparsely inhabited territory, and Theresa and Philippe, like virtually all of the Acadians in Maryland, had responded at once. Even Leon, whom the Ramseys had implored to stay, had insisted on leaving. The chance to be reunited with their families and to re-establish communities with their kin overrode all other considerations with the Acadians.

In many ways, the years of Theresa and Philippe's marriage had been good ones. They had been given a small frame house on the Ramsey property—unwhitewashed so that it would not compete in splendor with Leon's—and both of them had worked on the plantation. Philippe worked under

121

Leon, and Theresa continued to run the dispensary where she took care of sick slaves and served as midwife for the large bustling plantation. Nine months after they were reunited, a stillborn daughter was born, but then little Jacqueline arrived.

After he resigned himself to the loss of Theresa, Leon had received permission to travel to Annapolis for the purpose of finding an Acadian wife. The Ramseys were understandably distressed to discover that Leon's marriage to Theresa had been bigamous and was therefore not valid, but Leon had been able to convince them that he had sincerely believed Philippe to be dead. He had returned from Annapolis with a native of the Acadian town of Pisiquid named Claudine Bourque, who had proved to be an obedient, industrious, and fertile wife. Leon and Claudine were already the parents of three children. But for all those blessings, the Landrys and Bernards were still servants, isolated by culture and religion from the people around them. As she traveled her daily rounds of healing and homemaking, memories of her Acadian home and hearth were never far from Theresa's mind.

Except for the fortunate ones living in Baltimore, Annapolis, and Oxford—who had managed to find work and were relatively well treated—the Acadians in Maryland had found themselves despised outcasts, soon reduced to begging and penury. Many had died of starvation and disease.

As Theresa looked eagerly about the wharf, she recognized some of her old neighbors, but they had aged so that the sight of them saddened her. Still, there was the joy of speaking French with someone other than the members of her immediate family. When the *Virgin*'s anchor was raised and the ship's sails filled with wind and moved slowly out into Chesapeake Bay, Theresa's spirits soared at the prospect of the new life before her.

Philippe joined her at the ship's rail and put his arm around her, giving her shoulder an affectionate squeeze. "Why are you smiling?"

"I was thinking about the difference between this journey and the last one I took, and all that has happened in the years between."

When her father had caught her in the hayloft with Philippe, on that day that now seemed so long ago, it might have happened in another lifetime. Theresa had told her father that she was a woman. She knew now that it had not been so. She had had the body of a woman, and she had experienced the hunger that a woman feels for a man, but for all that, she had been little more than a child. She was a wife now, a woman grown, with a husband and child of her own. She had spent many a night soothing women who cried with the pain of giving birth and had experienced those pains herself. She had gazed with awe at her newborn children, filled with joy at the miracle of new life and pride that she had been able to create it. She had been moved with the wonder parents feel when they see that their offspring have fingers and toes and moving limbs and are, in fact, tiny, complete human beings. She had spent sleepless nights by the bedsides of her children when they were ill, filled with tender solicitude for their suffering and occasional terror for the outcome. She had increased her store of medical knowledge, and her reputation had grown until the Ramseys themselves asked her to attend them during their illnesses. She had seen many people meet death, some with terror, others with quiet strength or resignation, some with the serene conviction that another and better life awaited them. She had known the Ramseys and their friends, people who lived careless lives of aimless pleasure, and the McIntyres, who were tied together as firmly by the years they had spent tormenting each other as other married couples were tied together by love. She had seen the subterfuges and deceits that slaves practiced in their unending struggle with their masters, a struggle in which, in the end, there could be no victor. She had come to understand that in the end slavery was a system that destroyed master almost as brutally as it destroyed slave.

Philippe broke her reverie with a kiss on the top of her head. "Last time we left against our will; now we are going because we want to. We'll have our own land at last, and we will call no man our master. Just think—our own farm, our own home, freedom."

Theresa nestled against his shoulder. She had thought often of her father's gloomy prognostications about what life would offer her should she marry Philippe. So far, his fears had been groundless. Philippe worked hard to give her a decent life. He and Leon did not like each other, but by keeping their distance and taking care not to infringe on each other's prerogatives, they had arrived at a working relationship.

Leon's system of crop rotation had succeeded beyond his wildest hopes. The profits of the Ramsey plantation had risen so dramatically since Leon had become overseer that the other planters in the area began to take note, and soon they were turning to him for advice. Between his work for the Ramseys and a growing business as a consultant to the other planters of Talbot County, Leon found himself with more work than he could handle, and he was glad to use Philippe as his assistant. Philippe could communicate easily with people, a skill Leon lacked, and by treating the Ramseys' slaves as human beings, he had managed to get more work out of them than Leon had ever been able to do with his stiff air of command. Leon had come, at last, to have a grudging respect for Philippe, although he never forgave him for stealing Theresa.

Although he chafed under servitude, there was no question that Philippe was strong and determined. He seemed driven by a restless energy that never flagged, and from dawn to dark he was never still. He was fiercely devoted to his family. Jacqueline adored him, and no matter how long his work day, he always found some time to spend with her in the evening. His deepest love he reserved for Theresa. When he looked at her, he was like a child in her hands. He could never deny her a single thing she wanted if it was in his power to give it to her. He contrived to satisfy her love of finery with new clothes and an occasional piece of jewelry—how, she never knew—and when she was with child, he was somehow able to satisfy her cravings for strange food. When she asked him where he had found sour pickles, a rare delicacy for people in their station, or crabcakes when crabs were not in season, he would only smile mysteriously and tell her not to be so inquisitive.

With the security of his love about her like a cloak, Theresa lived her days in placid contentment. But her happiness was not complete. There was always the dream of seeing her parents again and having a home that she could truly call her own, and there were times when she would wake in the

124

middle of the night, trembling and frightened, haunted by strange dreams she could not remember. When she had such dreams, she would be overcome with a fear that her days of happiness with Philippe were numbered, that the years were a peaceful interlude between great catastrophes. Philippe would hold her until her trembling stopped, soothe her fears with gentle words, and stroke her back and shimmering hair until she went back to sleep. When Leon had relayed to Philippe the invititation from the territorial governor of Louisiana, he had accepted without even consulting Theresa, knowing there was no need.

The *Virgin* arrived in New Orleans on a warm day in early March. While the Acadian men, who had elected Leon as their leader, negotiated with Commissionaire Denis-Nicolas Foucault for supplies and drew up an agreement with a retired military officer named Antoine Bernard Dauterive to tend his cattle, Theresa roamed the streets of a town so low that mud seeped up between the cobblestones.

She loved New Orleans on sight. For the first time in ten years, she heard French spoken in the streets, although it was alternated with Spanish, a language she did not know. Moreover, the Creole French of Louisiana was spoken with an accent that fell strangely on her ears. In the harbor were boats laden with goods from France and Spain—cases of wine and perfume, boxes of china and silk, and little dolls dressed in the latest styles from the French court. Food of all kinds could be purchased in an open market by the wharf. Black women, singing of their wares in melodious voices, sold fruits and vegetables from large baskets that they carried on their heads. In the shops, imported goods competed with furs and belts of wampum from the wild trapping country to the North. Philippe was fascinated by the rough frontiersmen who poled their flatboats down the great Mississippi to sell their goods in New Orleans. These were rough, grizzled men, dressed in fur hats and buckskin, who swapped tall tales in their harsh twangy English and were looked upon with the greatest disdain by the haughty Creoles, as those people in Louisiana who had come directly from France and Spain were called.

125

Theresa gaped at the fashionable ladies of the town, who had a style not even the Ramseys could match. She had never seen so many pretty women—elegant Frenchwomen, dressed in the latest styles, and dark-skinned, velvet-eyed Spanish ladies, their hair covered by lacy black mantillas, who were carried in sedan chairs to the steps of the St. Louis Cathedral so that their dainty shoes would not be soiled. The ladies gossiped behind their fans, sipped strong coffee diluted with thick cream, and opened the windows of their homes onto their lacy ironwork balconies to enjoy the balmy spring air.

Theresa finally heard mass again in a real Catholic church, filled with other Catholics, instead of in a Protestant chapel on one of the rare occasions when a priest had come to see them. When the bells of the cathedral rang over the Place d'Armes, the sound filled her with joy, and she was sorry when the time came to leave.

The Acadians, their possessions supplemented by food, tools, muskets, ammunition, and building materials provided by Commissionaire Foucault, stepped into cumbersome *bateaux* and began their slow journey through the tortuous waterways of Louisiana to their new home in the Attakapas country. Up the churning brown waters of the Mississippi River they traveled to the Bayou Plaquemine, which, in turn, branched off into the Atchafalaya River. Under the guidance of Louis Andry, a military engineer, the Acadians negotiated a maze of waterways, leaving the Atchafalaya Basin until the Bayou Teche led them at last to the end of their journey, the Poste des Attakapas. At first, the bodies of water they traveled were broad, murky torrents, lined on either side by forests of trees that Theresa found familiar, but as their journey progressed, the bodies of water narrowed, and she entered a strange world.

Theresa had never imagined anything like the bayou country of Louisiana. The narrow waterways flowed languidly through a strange dreamlike world whose silence was broken during the day only by the song of a bird, the soft rustle of a small animal in the undergrowth along the banks, the plop of a snake from a branch, or the stealthy slithering of an alligator—a strange, crusted creature resembling a huge lizard that made little Jacqueline whimper in fear—as it slid into the

126

water. At night, the tree frogs shrilled, and the bayou bull-frogs croaked so loudly that Theresa had trouble sleeping at first, but she soon grew so accustomed to the sound that she hardly noticed it.

The Landrys and Bernards found themselves in a semitropical land with vegetation so dense that plants seemed to be struggling with each other for space to breathe. Lush palmettos and cypress trees grew so thick that the swamp lay always dim and moist. It was a land of dappled light and shadow and muted colors—gray water, gray moss, dull green leaves of live oak and cypress, pale lavender water hyacinths, gray lichen on the trunks of cypress trees. Only the ferns grew bright green, their fronds waving gently, as if in melancholy greeting. The cypress trees, their knobby roots thrusting out from the bank and clutching at the soil in a greedy tangle, reminded Theresa of old men. Everywhere the moss swayed mournfully, hanging from the cypresses like tattered clothing. ("Look, Mama," cried little Jacqueline, pointing. "The trees have beards!") The water hyacinths grew so thick that they choked the bayous and impeded the Acadians' progress. The men had to push through them, struggling to free their oars, swearing at the nuisance.

At the Poste des Attakapas, a fort originally built as protection against a tribe of Indians now departed, the Acadians were greeted briefly by a man whom Louis Andry introduced as Julien St. Clair. The Acadians stared impassively at the elegantly dressed gentlemen whose frock coat and wig looked strangely out of place in the bayou wilderness.

St. Clair had dressed carefully for the occasion to impress upon these yokels his importance as one of the leading men of the region. There were three Creole French families in the area—the Dauterives, the de la Houssayes, and the St. Clairs—and Julien St. Clair had reluctantly been pressed into service to speak a word or two to the Acadians, who had been brought to the region to tend the Creoles' cattle. By the terms of the agreement drawn up in New Orleans, the Acadians, or Cajuns, as they soon came to be called, were obligated to tend a portion of the Creoles' herds for six years, in return for one-half of the increase. They had been given, in addition, grants of land and the supplies provided by Commissionaire Foucault.

Julien St. Clair looked at the poorly dressed peasants before him, drew a perfumed lace handkerchief from his coat, and sniffed it in delicate disgust. He had no idea how to address such creatures in terms they could understand. Sensing at once his condescension, the Acadians regarded him with solemn faces, but their eyes mocked him. They had had enough of superior airs in Maryland. Here they were free—and determined to be their own masters.

Only Leon Landry accepted St. Clair's own evaluation of himself. As the informally elected leader of the band of Acadians, he stepped forward and bowed. "Monsieur St. Clair, allow me to present Leon Landry," said Louis Andry, preforming the introductions.

"Delighted, I'm sure," said St. Clair, with the slightest nod in Leon's direction.

"Let me say what a pleasure it is for us to be here and how we look forward to making new homes in Louisiana and having such distinguished neighbors," said Leon to fill the silence, as St. Clair appeared to be at a loss for words.

"The pleasure is mutual," said St. Clair, annoyed that Leon had referred to him as "neighbor" rather than "master" or at least "employer." "May you be loyal and trustworthy servants, and I am sure the agreement into which we have entered will benefit all parties."

His reference to the Acadians as "servants" was not lost upon them. A ripple of laughter passed through the crowd. Little did Julien St. Clair suspect that Vincent Broussard, who stood behind him, was mimicking his every gesture. Vincent stood with one foot outthrust, gazing about him with the same patronizing air adopted by the Creole. When St. Clair sniffed his scented handkerchief, Vincent lifted imaginary lace to one nostril, his little finger crooked daintily, and inhaled. When St. Clair bowed, Vincent bowed. Although Leon shot him a look of reproach, the other Acadians, able to contain themselves no longer, crowed with delight. As soon as St. Clair, following their eyes, turned about, Vincent Broussard relaxed into his normal stance, eyes innocent, face a blank mask.

Julien St. Clair's face reddened. Insolent beggars! He knew

that they were mocking him, but he did not know how. "That will be all," he said stiffly, and with another small bow toward Leon, he stalked, stiff backed, into the fort.

"Oh, my dear Madame Allain," said Vincent Broussard in an affected drawl as soon as St. Clair had left, "may I have the pleasure of this dance?"

"Honored, I'm sure," Antonia Allain replied with a coy simper, fluttering an imaginary fan and cutting her eyes at Vincent in a most provocative manner. Vincent bowed deeply from the waist, Antonia gave him her best curtsy, and then, to the glee of the other Acadians, the two began executing a dainty minuet.

"Enough of such foolishness," Leon said, embarrassed that Andry should have seen such a discourteous display. "We've work to do if we want to have houses and food. Planting season is already upon us, and we have yet to plow a single furrow."

Under the guidance of Louis Andry, the Cajuns set to work at once to build their first homes, a task that consumed their first few days. The *poteaux ex terra* style from old Acadia, in which homes had been set on timbers driven into the ground, was not appropriate in the hot, humid climate of Louisiana, as the timbers would have quickly rotted. After sufficient trees had been felled, the heavy, hand-hewn timbers were erected into a crude frame, heavy studs resting on hand-hewn sills. Crosspieces were wedged between the studs and the gaps filled with a mixture of clay and moss. When the time came to fill the gaps, Andry instructed the Cajuns to dig a pit and fill it with loose clay. The clay was moistened with water from the bayou and quantities of moss were dumped on top. Then, removing their shoes, the men jumped into the pit and trampled the mixture until it reached the desired consistency. Theresa laughed at Philippe, who leaped into the pit with a loud shout and jumped about as if he were dancing, his red head aflame in the warm spring sun. He kept the morale of the other men high by turning work into play.

After the mixture was daubed into the spaces between the studs, a roof of handsplit shingles and a floor of roughly hewn boards were laid. With the addition of a mud chimney, the house was ready to be occupied. Like Acadian homes in

129

Nova Scotia, Theresa's new house had a steep roof, needed now to shed water instead of snow. The roof also created a roomy attic where future children could sleep. The Bernard home had a porch that extended the length of the house, on which Theresa could take her ease and enjoy the evening breeze when her work was done.

While the men helped each other put the finishing touches on their houses, Theresa hitched their new plow to a mule and turned a few clumsy furrows. She then planted the seeds, cuttings, and roots she had brought from Maryland and tended so carefully on the long journey. She did not know if the plants would thrive in the Louisiana soil, but she was sure that she would learn of other local herbs with healing properties. She knew she could not be happy with her garden until it sprouted her precious herbs.

At the end of the day on which their home was finished, Theresa sat on her porch with Philippe, surveying their new domain with pleasure. Little Jacqueline, with the easy adaptability of small children, was already at home, running around the yard with the inexhaustible energy of toddlers. She lifted her knees high as she ran about in circles, staring intently at the ground. Theresa had just returned from drawing water from the bayou and was tired, but content. She had her family about her, safe and in good health. She had property that was hers at last, a plot of earth she could call her own, and her own house. She even had the beginnings of a garden.

A shadow passed over her face. "What is it, *chère?*" asked Philippe, sensing the change in her mood.

"I was only thinking that if my parents and brothers and sisters were here, my happiness would be complete."

"They'll come; don't worry. We're the first to arrive, but there will be Acadians from all over the colonies down here before you know it." He waved his hand at the prospect before them. "This will be the New Acadia."

Theresa took his hand and smiled. "I like that. The New Acadia."

Chapter Sixteen

Nothing could have prepared Theresa for the July heat in Louisiana. It was wet, steamy heat that left Theresa's hands clammy and her clothing and linen damp. She remembered the previous summer, their first summer in Louisiana, and shook her head at the knowledge that August and September would be even worse. During those months of their first year, she had been nauseous and dizzy from the heat, with a dull, throbbing headache that sometimes lasted for days, until the sun had come to seem almost like a personal enemy. She even blamed the heat for the miscarriage she had suffered in August. During the worst of it, she had risen before first light to get as much work done as she could before the heat hit her; she could weed her garden in the dark, having learned to distinguish by touch the tender shoots of her herbs and flowers from the choking weeds that flourished so vigorously in the rich, moist soil. But except for the summers, she loved the climate—early fall and spring were glorious, and the winters so mild that the Acadians, accustomed to a harsher climate, rarely suffered.

Summer was the rainy season, Theresa learned, and with luck the rain cooled the earth, but at other times, the sun came out right after the rain and turned the moisture to steam.

When that happened, one could only hope for a breeze to lift the heat. At times, even the evenings brought no respite, but more often a fresh breeze would spring up in the late afternoon. The Bernards took full advantage of these Gulf breezes from the south, sitting on their porch until the mosquitoes drove them in and breathing in the sweet scent of the two cape jasmine plants Theresa had planted on either side of the walk leading to the house. There were other flowers, too—roses and lilies, zinnias and marigolds—but it was the heavy scent of jasmine which her family always associated with their home. Thick strands of moss on the live oak tree that sheltered the Bernard house swayed gently in the breeze.

On many evenings, the Bernards would simply sit and talk. The talk was as often of their old home in Acadia as of their new—Theresa and Philippe spoke to their daughter of their former life and of their families, with whom they still hoped to be reunited. "You would love your Aunt Claire. We were very close," Theresa would say. "She was only a year younger than I, and so pretty and gay!"

"Not as pretty as you," Philippe would interject. "Jacqueline, your mother was the prettiest girl in Grand Pré."

"Oh, no," said Theresa, blushing. "You just never noticed the others. My older sister Alice was the quiet one," she continued, "so quiet she sometimes got lost in the shuffle. But she was very good. Alice was so religious we all thought she would become a nun, but she married Arnaud Dugas instead. I can't wait for you to meet your grandfather. There was a man for you! My father was the best man in the world. You'll see for yourself when you meet him."

"He certainly didn't like me!" Philippe interposed.

"Why not?" asked Jacqueline, mesmerized by her parents' wonderful tales.

"He didn't think I was good enough for your mother. Her family was rich, and mine wasn't."

"That wasn't it. I don't think he would have thought anyone was good enough for me. Besides, I was young—only sixteen. The day before the men were locked up, Papa told me if I still wanted to marry you in a year, he would let me."

Then Jacqueline would clamor to hear the story of how the Acadians had been imprisoned by the English, how Philippe had escaped from the *Dolphin*, and how her mother had almost drowned to get onto his ship, only to discover that he was no longer on it. She never seemed to tire of the story, and she always wanted it to be told in exactly the same way.

She was a good child, Theresa thought, looking at her eager face. Philippe, who had a fine sense of drama and was better at telling stories than Theresa, told his daughter once again the tale of how he and Theresa had been reunited. Jacqueline was growing into a beautiful young girl and was spoiled by her father, so that Theresa sometimes felt compelled to be harsh with the child so she would not grow up totally undisciplined.

When Theresa looked out over their property, she often thought of what her father had said to her about love of the land. It had made little sense to her when she was younger, but she understood it very well now. Instead of living in the village of La Manque (which the settlement around the Poste des Attakapas was called before the name was changed to St. Martinville) and cultivating plots of outlying land in the European manner, the Acadians, fiercely territorial people that they were, had fenced in and established their own separate domains. Now there was a chain of dwellings between La Manque and La Pointe, which was later called Pont Breaux, or Breaux Bridge.

Theresa took great pride in their property. In the year and a half they had been in Louisiana, she and Philippe had labored long and hard to carve a home out of the wild, beautiful bayou country, which Theresa had come to love after she grew accustomed to its strangeness. She appreciated the land more as their first spring progressed, and the wild flowers—bright blue fleur-de-lis, red hibiscus, and beautiful orange and white striped spider lilies—bloomed in profusion and brought color to the muted gray and green and silver of the bayou. The birds, which seemed to be everywhere—cardinals, blue jays, thrushes, blackbirds, redheaded woodpeckers—she loved, too, even when they woke the Bernards at dawn with their raucous voices.

It was a land of plenty. The bayous were full of perch and catfish; Jacqueline soon learned to capture the small but succulent lobsterlike crawfish. After Philippe had plowed the soft earth, he was amazed at the rapidity with which their first crops sprang up—corn and rice from the seed stock he had brought from New Orleans, vegetables, and a small patch of cotton. Then there were fences to be constructed, furniture to be made to supplement the pieces they had brought with them, and enclosures to be built for their animals. Besides the cattle, Philippe had been given one rooster, six hens, two sows and a pig, two geese and a gander, two mules, and a horse.

After they had taken care of the first necessities of building their new homes, the Acadians had begun slowly to re-establish their old communities. Narcisse LeBlanc, who had been the best fiddler in Grand Pré, lived halfway between La Manque and La Pointe, and with the help of his neighbors, he constructed a dance hall that was within traveling distance of both towns. The Saturday night dances drew Cajuns from miles around. Theresa loved to dance, and on such occasions she almost felt like a girl again. Despite the striking differ-ence in the physical environments of the new and old Acadias, there were times when Theresa heard her neighbors chattering away in French and the familiar tunes from the old country played on violin and accordion that she almost forgot the trauma of the intervening years and felt that she was back in her old home. Neighbors who were within easy traveling distance visited with each other often.

Theresa's most frequent guest was Leon's wife, Claudine, who lived in the next house and frequently came to sit with Theresa in the evening. Claudine was only a year older than Theresa, but she had had a child almost every year since her marriage and had already grown stout; to Theresa, she seemed years older. For a long time, Leon had been reluctant to tell Claudine of the year he had spent with Theresa, assuming that his wife would resent it, but when he finally did confess that he had inadvertently been involved in a brief bigamous mar-riage with his cousin, Claudine shrugged it off. It did not lessen the affection she felt for Theresa; nothing mattered to Claudine except that she was now Leon's lawful wife. He was a good provider and the acknowledged leader of the Acadians, and Claudine was proud to be married to him.

Theresa's greatest regret was that there was no one to give

her child religious instruction. The only Catholic priests in the region were two missionaries, one from Natchitoches and one from Pointe Coupee, each of whom made a visit to La Manque about every three months to say mass, perform marriages, and baptize infants. Their visits were eagerly anticipated, as much for the news they brought from other Acadian communities as for the spiritual comfort they provided. The Acadians had wanted to settle all in the same area so that as new shiploads from the English colonies came in, it would be easy for family members to find each other and re-establish ties of kinship, but the first Spanish governor of Louisiana, Antonio de Ulloa, had different ideas. A portion of Louisiana east of the Mississippi River had been transferred to England, leaving the Catholic territory vulnerable on its eastern border. Against the vigorous protests of the Acadians, Ulloa decided to spread the incoming Acadians out along this border for reasons of defense. Thus scattered, it was a number of years before they were able to be together as they wished, and they relied on trappers, tradesmen, men driving cattle to New Orleans and other points on the Mississippi, and the priests in the area to carry news from one settlement to another.

The two priests who visited the Attakapas communities during their earliest days could not have been more unlike each other. Father Batiste, from Natchitoches, was short and stout, with a balding head, red complexion, and a brisk, energetic manner. He loved good food and good company. Had there been a trace of malice in his constitution, he would have been considered a gossip, but it was only his love of people that made him remember in great detail and relate with such relish the events of birth, marriage, and death, of good and bad harvest, and other turns in the fortunes of the Cajuns up and down the Mississippi and along the network of bayous.

The other Priest, Father Verret, was of medium height and as lean as Father Batiste was stout. His dark hair was close-cropped, and he had sharp features, a sallow complexion, and bright, almost feverish black eyes that peered out from behind heavy-hooded lids. Saturnine and laconic, he seemed to be hiding some heavy sorrow behind his air of quiet melancholy. He was a mysterious figure to the Cajuns, respected but not loved. They were surprised to hear that he was a Jesuit and a

135

man of great learning. Why such a man should be in such a primitive wilderness when he should more likely have been found poring over Greek and Latin texts in some European library was the subject of considerable conjecture. He had perhaps offended the church hierarchy in some serious way to have been thus banished—but what could his offense have been? He was not a man of violent temper, given to the kind of outbursts that might have alienated his superiors; he seemed to have great self-control, and whatever his sins, they were almost certainly not those of the flesh. It was impossible to imagine him a womanizer, and he ate and drank sparingly. At any rate, here he was, and the Cajuns came simply to accept him. Whereas everyone was on the friendliest terms with Father Batiste and vied for the privilege of his company, no one was close to Father Verret with the possible exception of Leon Landry, with whom the priest, during his visits to the area, sat up late into the night discussing books.

The Cajuns' second year in Louisiana was more relaxed than the first, as life settled into a routine dictated by the demands of the seasons. There was not much work for the men to do in the hottest months of summer except to gather wood for the brief winter. During July and August, cattle and crops more or less took care of themselves, but Theresa's work was never finished. Even when her daily housework was completed, there was always spinning on the wheel she had brought from Maryland or weaving on the loom Philippe had made for her. Her special pride, her flower and herb garden, required a good bit of tending.

She had acquired her first flowers from the St. Clair garden, whose beauty she had admired greatly from the first time she saw it. She was at first afraid to approach the house, so grand did it seem beside the crude dwellings of the Acadians. Philippe, who did not consider any man alive to be better than he, could not understand her hesitation, but it was several weeks after their arrival in Louisiana before Theresa summoned the nerve to approach the St. Clair estate.

The two-story house was pink, with a black iron staircase curving up on either side to the second floor gallery. A magnificent cutglass fanlight stood over the front door, which had a handle and knocker of polished brass. A wrought-iron fence surrounded the house and grounds and prevented Theresa from getting close enough to see the interior. But through the heavy drapes of blue brocade, held back with tasseled cords, she could catch glimpses of black and white marble mantels, mirrors with gilded frames, and walls adorned with heavy silver candle sconces. But for all of the house's grandeur, it was the garden that drew her eye again and again.

When at last Theresa stepped through the wide front gate, it was into a yard filled with fragrant trees—mimosa, banana, and magnolia, as well as moss-draped oaks—and brick-bordered gardens full of rose and azalea bushes, oleanders, fragrant jasmine and gardenias, delicate camellias, waxy lilies, and fiery hibiscus. She walked around to the back of the house, lacking the courage to mount the stairs and lift the heavy brass knocker.

A black woman emerged from one of a row of small slave houses. She and Theresa stopped and looked each other over from head to toe, each taking the other's measure. The woman was pretty, with light brown skin, broad cheekbones, and a full mouth. "May I help you?" she called to Theresa at last.

"Yes," Theresa responded shyly. "My name is Theresa Bernard. My husband and I have just moved here, and I was admiring your garden. I was wondering if you might let me have a few seeds and cuttings so that I might start one of my own."

The woman smiled. Although she was a slave, she carried herself with pride and confidence, her head held high, and she spoke excellent French. "I'm sure no one would mind. My name is Lena."

This was the beginning of an association that was to prove of great value to Theresa. Lena not only helped Theresa start her garden, but she gave her invaluable advice on the special aspects of Louisiana housekeeping. She showed Theresa how to erect a frame over her bed on which mosquito netting could be draped and how to make a salve to soothe mosquito bites. She showed her how to dry sassafras leaves to make the powdered filé that seasoned the thick rich stews the slaves called gumbo. She gave Theresa arsenic to kill the grasshoppers and other insects that crept into the Bernards' house in the summer and showed her how to protect against bedbugs by taking her beds apart twice a year and treating the cracks with a mixture of quicksilver and egg white. She gave Theresa bricks to line either side of the walk leading up to her home, but Theresa insisted on paying for them with eggs as soon as her hens started laying.

Theresa enjoyed talking to Lena, and the women were soon friends. In the colonies, the Acadians had been treated no better, and often worse, than their employees' slaves, who were, after all, valuable and expensive pieces of property; it was not until they had been in Louisiana for many years that the Cajuns began to develop racial prejudices. Indeed, their absence of prejudice was a source of concern to their employers in the colonies, who were afraid that their slaves would develop independent notions as a result of being treated as equals by the Frenchmen. Lena, although cool and skeptical at first, soon realized that Theresa's friendly manner was not an affectation and began to look forward to her visits.

On one of her first visits, Theresa was observed from a window by Julien St. Clair, who noted in passing that the Cajun housewife with the sweet smile, mass of black curls, and large dark eyes was a pretty little thing. He thought idly that she might be good for a few evenings' diversion should his other resources fail him. He had only been there for a few years, but already the amusements available to him were beginning to pall, and the ennui of life in the country was rapidly becoming as oppressive as the wet, sticky heat.

He shook his head, saddened that he should be reduced to even contemplating a liaison with a peasant's wife. That he, Julien St. Clair, who had been the intimate of marchionesses and the darling of countesses, should have come to such a pass! He took a pinch of snuff from a silver box, sniffed it, and sneezed delicately into a lace handkerchief. "Ah, that I should have been consigned to the provinces by a noble father, and all for a few youthful indiscretions!" he said aloud with a sigh, noting with a practiced eye the full curve of Theresa's breasts and her narrow waist. I'll bet she has a trim ankle, too, he thought; for all that, she has no more breeding than the slave she engages in conversation so intimately. He could not abide women with large feet and thick ankles.

138

That he had wound up in the provinces through the actions of an aristocratic father was one of a number of fictions Julien St. Clair had invented. Although the handful of Creole families in the Attakapas region gave themselves airs and to a man considered themselves too fine to lift a hand at any form of honest labor, the truth was that most of them had embroidered considerably upon their family trees. It was a simple fact that wealthy people whose positions in society were secure did not emigrate; why should one risk the hazards of life in a raw, untamed country unless one had his fortune to make? Alphonse de la Houssaye, it is true, had been made a chevalier by the king and could therefore lay modest claim to a title; but Julien St. Clair's claims to connections at court and references to weekends spent at Versailles were complete fabrications.

He had been born Julien Chauvin, the illegitimate son of a tavern maid. His father was an itinerant actor who had passed through the village of Chardonet in the spring of 1732, sowing a seed that he never even knew had borne fruit. His only legacies to his son were a handsome profile, a way with women, and a flair for the histrionic, the last of which Julien had used to his advantage when he left Chardonet at the age of eighteen to try his fortune as an actor in Paris. He enjoyed little success on the stage, but his good looks enabled Julien to become the companion of a succession of rich, bored women whose husbands neglected them. In Paris, he picked up the social graces that allowed him to pass as a gentleman, and it was there that he canonized himself by changing his name to St. Clair.

A confrontation with an irate husband when Julien was twenty-eight, from which he barely escaped with his life, persuaded him that his days in Paris were numbered. He had begun looking to the future, when he could no longer rely solely on his looks and charm for a living. What he needed was a rich wife, but his chances of acquiring one in Paris were remote. So, in 1760, he sailed to New Orleans with little more than a fashionable wardrobe and a few pieces of good jewelry with fond inscriptions from patronesses whose names he had already forgotten. By selling his jewelry and acquiring a wealthy mistress, he was able to survive until he managed to win the heart of Sidonie Girard, a sheltered girl of good family who had just completed her education at the Ursuline Convent. Julien told Sidonie that he was the younger son of a nobleman who, having become angered at Julien's boyish escapades, had sent his wayward son to New Orleans to prove that he could survive on his own merits. He led her to believe that should he be reinstated in his father's good graces, he would be heir to a considerable fortune. Not only did the naive young girl believe every word he told her, but his youthful exploits only served to enhance his attractiveness in Sidonie's eyes. She thought his life to be glamorous and full of adventure and hers dull and uneventful by comparison. She listened to his tales so avidly that he began embellishing them even more extravagantly to please her, and he told these lies so frequently that in the end he came to believe them himself.

Sidonie's father saw through Julien at once, but to his horror, his daughter insisted that if she were not allowed to marry Julien, she would take the veil. Clement Girard was in a quandary. Should he forbid Sidonie a dowry, he was convinced that the child would be either abused by Julien St. Clair or doomed to convent life. He knew Julien was a fortune hunter and an adventurer and could not bear to watch his good money going to support such a scoundrel. He compromised by giving Sidonie a smaller dowry and a tract of land in the Attakapas region. Knowing that the last thing Julien St. Clair would wish was to be stuck in the country, Girard made it part of the marriage contract that his child live there. Sidonie, after several years of marriage, which produced a daughter, realized her mistake and turned to the consolation of religion, making frequent retreats to the convent where she had been educated. This left Julien, for the most part, to his own devices. He had grown tired of amusing himself with the slave women, and the only married woman in the area he found desirable had succumbed so quickly to his advances that she bored him almost as soon as she had been conquered.

This was the impasse at which he found himself when Theresa came into his view. Shortly after, the new Creole families moving into the area from Mobile and Fort Toulouse, which had recently been taken over by the British, offered him fresh sources of diversion. So for a full year and a half Theresa was spared his attentions. But now it was July again, with the blazing sun turning his house into an inferno and his wife and daughter in New Orleans, and once again Julien St. Clair was bored, restless, and ready for adventure.

Chapter Seventeen

During the last week of July and the first week of August, the men had their hardest work of the summer—felling trees and cutting and splitting logs for the stacks of cordword behind each farmhouse. The farmer's *bûcher*, or woodpile, ensured that his family would not go cold that winter and that his wife's cooking fires would be well stoked throughout the coming year. The men loved their annual *bûcherie*, as it allowed them some time alone together in the deep, quiet wooded areas close to their farms. It was a community affair during which the men showed off their skill with the ax and crosscut saw, while the women took turns providing a hearty midday repast. Then, during the hottest hours of the day, the men would nap, gossip, or smoke before returning to work.

It was late on one such afternoon that Theresa received an unexpected visit from Father Batiste. She would always remember with great clarity the scene into which he stepped although it was one of the most ordinary domestic nature. Jacqueline was responsible for feeding the barnyard animals, and Theresa had already shucked and shelled corn for the chickens and geese. Theresa was under a tree, hulling rice by pounding it in her wooden mortar with a pestle made from a gum-tree pole. Jacqueline, who loved to throw handfuls of corn in a wide circle, squatted in the dirt and shouted, "Here, chicky, chicky!" The chickens ran right and left in circles, clucking with greedy excitement, while the geese honked and hissed and jockeyed for positions close to Jacqueline. The pigs, not to be outdone, emitted such raucous squeals that Theresa threw them each an ear of corn to shut them up. While Jacqueline tossed the corn—now here, now there, so that the fowl had to run hither and thither to catch it, stepping on each other in their haste—Theresa stopped her hulling long enough to fill the pigs' trough with leftovers from the kitchen. The pigs grunted and sucked up their slops as if they had not eaten in days, trying to shove each other out of the way with their snouts and eat at the same time.

It was into this scene that Father Batiste stepped, going around to the back of the house when he saw no one inside. He smiled fondly at the serious intensity with which Jacqueline approached her task and asked Theresa if he might have a word with her. Theresa got up from her work at once and invited the priest inside, grateful that only that morning she had scrubbed her floor with fresh water and a twig broom.

"I think I have located some of your relatives," he said after Theresa had offered him a cool drink and their best chair.

"Oh, have you found my father?" she cried, clasping her hands before her and bouncing up and down on her chair like a child.

"No, not your father. Do you have a sister named Claire? Was your mother's name Marie-Jeanne Landry?"

"Yes, yes! Where are they?"

"Living near the military post at Cabannoce. They came in on a ship from Pennsylvania. Your sister married a man named Roland Olivier in Pennsylvania, and they have three children."

"Claire has three children?" Theresa laughed at the thought. "What are their names?"

"She has a girl and two boys. The girl is called Theresa, for you. The boys are called Jean Baptiste and Germain. Germain is just an infant—about nine months old."

It was only later that Theresa thought to marvel at Father Batiste's remarkable memory. "Wait until Jacqueline hears that she has so many cousins! And my mother—her health is good?"

"For an old woman, yes. She is doing about as well as can be expected."

"My mother isn't an old woman!"

"My dear, you haven't seen her in a long time," the priest said gently.

"Yes, you're right." Her mother, whom Theresa remembered as so vigorous, now an old woman!

"Your brothers Claude and René were put on different ships. Claire heard that Claude is alive, but she cannot be sure it is true. Nothing is known of René. The little boys did not survive the journey from Nova Scotia."

"Evariste and Richard are dead?"

The poor little boys. Theresa always thought of her family exactly as it had been before they left. She thought of Claire as a young girl, and now she was a married woman with three children! There was one name the priest had not mentioned. She was almost afraid to say it.

"And my father?"

"Dead, too, I'm afraid. He died two years after your family was sent to Pennsylvania."

"No, it's impossible. There must be some mistake," she cried.

"I'm sorry, my dear. I heard it from your mother's lips."

Her father, dead for years! And for all of these years she had thought him alive, imagined their reunion. She twisted her hands in her lap, trying to choke back her emotions.

"Would you like me to pray with you?" asked the priest, responding to her distress.

"No, I must be alone." She knew she was going to cry and did not want anyone to see her.

"Why don't I tell Jacqueline you're going for a walk?"

"Yes, that would be good of you," said Theresa, rising and stumbling blindly for the door, hardly aware of what she was doing.

"And I will pray for your father's soul."

Theresa nodded and ran out the door, down the brick-lined walk, and out into the woods. She headed in the direction of the St. Clair house, knowing it was a path rarely used. As

144

soon as she was out of sight of her home, she sank down onto the stump of a tree, buried her face in her hands, and burst into tears. She was a woman grown, with a child of her own, but at the news of her father's death, she felt suddenly like a child herself, an orphan, bereft of hope, helpless, desolate. She thought over and over again how strange it was that her father could have been dead for so many years when she had thought that he was alive. How could he not be?

She knew then that the rituals of mourning are for the living. The wake and prayers and candles, the requiem mass and solemn interment—all were for the living, a farewell ceremony to drive home the reality of death and loss. She had been cheated of those rituals, cheated of her farewell. She had not seen her father's body lain out in his best clothes. She had put no flowers on his grave. He had been buried on foreign soil, in a strange place called Pennsylvania, far from the bones of his ancestors and the home that he had loved. She rocked back and forth, weeping for the father she would never see again.

She remembered, suddenly, the time he had taken her with him to inspect the dikes. He had looked at his children and said, "Now which one of you would like to go with me?" They had all waved their hands, dancing about and shouting, "Me, me! Take me, Papa!" Only Theresa had remained silent, her large dark eyes fixed on her father's face, breathless with longing.

"I'll take Theresa," he said, and had picked her up, swinging her high onto the broad back of his horse. How important she had felt, because her father was an important man, and he had chosen her. Now she felt that she was no longer important or loved or anyone at all.

Who was she? Where was she? She looked about at the moss-draped trees and wild, lush vegetation she had grown to love, and they all seemed suddenly foreign, sinister and predatory. She was completely disoriented. She wanted to rage against something for the smashed families and burned homes, for the ravaged hopes and severed lives of her people. Someone, surely, was to blame for all of this destruction. Her anger was not directed at the English. She felt, vaguely, that there was something larger involved, that the Acadians had been swept away by some rapid, treacherous current of history that she could not understand and that no one could control. Or perhaps history was not the right word for it. She thought perhaps that they had all been smashed by some giant cosmic fist.

As she sat struggling with these thoughts, a hand fell on her shoulder. She looked up to see Julien St. Clair looming over her. He smiled down at her, thinking that her sorrow and helplessness made her even more attractive.

"Madame Bernard, is it not?"

"Why, yes," she said, wiping her tear-stained cheeks with the back of her hand and smoothing her dress, embarrassed.

"I don't believe we've had the pleasure of meeting. I'm Julien St. Clair."

"Oh, I know who you are! I've been to your house several times. Lena has been kind enough to help me with my garden," Theresa replied as she stood.

"Yes, I've seen you talking to her. I hope you have everything you need?"

"Oh, yes, she's been very kind."

"Let me know if there is anything which she cannot supply, and I will be more than glad to assist you."

"You're very kind."

"I don't mean to pry, but you seem to be in distress. May I be of any help?"

"I'm afraid I've just received some bad news."

"How very distressing," he said, his voice as smooth as silk. "We are only a short distance from my home. Perhaps a glass of wine would help to revive your spirits."

"I really should be getting home. I left my daughter unattended," she said, glancing down the road toward her home.

"Surely you would not wish her to see you in such a disturbed state," he said, shrewdly guessing that it was why she was out crying in the woods in the first place.

"Yes, you're right. Perhaps I should attempt to compose myself before going home."

"Come along now and tell me all about it." Julien St. Clair took her elbow and escorted her through the woods to his estate. Deceived by the look of deep concern on his face and his murmured words of sympathy, Theresa found herself telling him about her life in Nova Scotia, her father, and her distress on hearing of his death and those of her little brothers. She was not in the habit of discussing such matters with strangers, but she could not talk to Philippe until he got in from the woods that evening, and St. Clair had caught her at an unusually vulnerable moment.

Inside the St. Clair home, Julien rang a bell for a servant and ordered a bottle of wine and two glasses. The wine was strong but deceptively smooth, and in her agitation, Theresa drank too much. Julien, who sipped his glass slowly and filled Theresa's as rapidly as she drained it, watched her carefully and noted the flush that rose to her cheeks and the slight slur in her speech. He was not, of course, listening to a word she said, but he maintained a look of the utmost solicitude and said, "How dreadful," and, "Please do continue," and, "What happened next?" at what appeared to be appropriate moments.

Theresa at last stopped talking, suddenly embarrassed that she had confided in a stranger. "I shouldn't have told you all this," she said shyly. "I'm sure it can't be of any interest to you."

"Quite to the contrary, my dear. I found it most fascinating. Such an unusual life you have led! How many hardships you have borne, and with such bravery!"

He filled her glass again. "How many times I have observed you from my window and longed to make your acquaintance! I suspected that you were a remarkable woman as well as a beautiful one, and now I find my expectations more than satisfied. I wonder if your husband knows what a treasure he possesses?"

"Oh, yes, Philippe and I could not be happier," Theresa said. She was at last truly uncomfortable. "Speaking of Philippe, I really must be getting home. It's time for supper." She rose to leave.

Julien St. Clair rose and took her by the shoulders. "Not so hastily, I beg you. I have so looked forward to having a moment alone with you! I cannot bear for it to end so soon. A woman like you should not have to do her own housework.

Really, my dear, you should have servants of your own. It could easily be arranged, you know, were you to wish it.''

Theresa ran for the door, angry at herself for having been such a fool as to confide in this man. He was too quick for her, however, and reached the door a step ahead of her. He put his back against the wall and drew her to him. Grasping her hair in his hand, he forced her head back and gave her a deep, lingering kiss.

Theresa struggled to free herself, but he was a powerful man and had his mouth on hers so firmly that she could not speak. Finally, he released her head but grasped her firmly by both shoulders. "I've wanted you for so long," he whispered. "I've waited and waited for you."

"Let me go!" she demanded, pale with fury. "How could you be so despicable, taking advantage of me at such a moment!" She beat his chest with her hands.

The struggle only served to excite him. He grasped her hair again and pulled it back until her neck was arched and she cried out from the pain. "A little Cajun wildcat!" he said, laughing softly. "We shall see who can tame you."

He bent down and began kissing her throat, pulling her back by the hair until Theresa thought that she would choke. Reaching blindly for his face, she raked her nails down his cheek.

Julien St. Clair grabbed his face, swearing, and struck Theresa in the face with his other hand. "I'll teach you to fight me!" he said, and pushed her roughly to the floor. Theresa kicked and screamed with all her might, and with a sickening feeling, she heard the side seam of her bodice tear. Julien St. Clair was suprised at the strength in her small frame, but her resistance served only to arouse him. Clawing and beating her assailant like a tiger, Theresa succeeded finally in bringing her knee up into his groin. He doubled over, clutching himself, and in the moment's freedom she was given, Theresa leaped to her feet and ran out of the house as fast as she could.

It was now dark. Theresa ran for home, able to think of nothing but the shelter of her husband's arms. Philippe, home from the woods, heard her footsteps on the path and came out to meet her. Without a word, he put his arms around her.

"I saw Father Batiste. I'm so sorry, Theresa, so very sorry."

She buried her face in his chest and began sobbing again. "Sh, sh," he soothed her, patting her back and leading her back down the path, away from their home.

"I must feed Jacqueline," she said, choking on her sobs.

"I've already done it. I think we need a little time alone." They walked until they found a quiet spot in the woods and sat down.

"I always suspected that your father was dead. He wasn't a young man when we were deported, and men like him, who are older and settled and have deep roots, don't transplant easily. But I couldn't say anything to you—you always talked so eagerly about seeing him again."

"It's not just the deaths. I keep thinking about the wrecked lives and ruined homes and twisted fortunes of all of us." She told him all that she had thought in the woods before Julien St. Clair found her.

Philippe listened to her gravely. "I know you think often about Grand Pré and how happy you were there. It's as if we had all been kicked out of the garden of Eden. But Theresa, it wasn't that wonderful. You've just built it up in your mind because you were a child and protected and happy. Most people look back on their childhoods that way. But there were plenty of people in the old country who were sick or unhappily married or discontented with their lots. It wasn't the paradise you think it was."

"No, but it was a good life, don't you think? A simple life but a good one. I know I tend to romanticize it, but I can't help comparing the family I grew up in to the McIntyres and the Ramseys and even the rich people down here, and it seems to me that we were happier. If we had stayed in Acadia, we could have been married, and our children could have known their grandparents, and all of this death and devastation would never have occurred."

Philippe chuckled. "I don't think it would have been that simple. I don't think life every really proceeds along a straight course for very long. It seems to twist and jump around. Happiness and order seem to come and go in spurts, however carefully we lay our plans."

"You don't think we would have been happy in Grand Pré?"

Philippe was silent for a moment, reflecting. "I'm not sure. I've often thought about the things your father said about me. He was by no means a stupid man, and there was some truth in his assessment."

"Oh, no," Theresa interrupted. "That's one of the main reasons I'm so sorry he's dead. I always wanted him to know how happy we've been together and how wrong he was about you. He was just jealous because you were taking me away from him."

Philippe plucked a blade of grass and began pulling it apart slowly. "The men in my family do have a wild, rambunctious streak. I think we were made to live in places like this." He waved one arm in a wide arc. "I think we're frontier people. We like to have plenty of room to move around in. The Bernards need breathing space, or we feel cooped up, and then we start smashing things. Put us down in a settled community, and we seem to go a little crazy. I think I'm a lot happier, and a lot better to you and Jacqueline, than I would have been if we hadn't been deported."

Theresa digested this in silence. These things had never occurred to her, and she was surprised that Philippe had thought them out so carefully. She thought of him as a man of action who seldom troubled himself with such deep reflections.

"I'm already starting to feel hemmed in. Too many people are moving into the area. How would you feel about moving west?" He had taken a few steps away from Theresa, and his back was to her.

"I don't know. I'll have to think about it." The day before she would have been reluctant to start over after they had worked so hard to get settled, but now she was disturbed by the proximity of Julien St. Clair.

Philippe turned. "We've got plenty of time to think about it." He reached over and kissed her cheek on the spot where Julien St. Clair had struck her. A bruise was forming, and Theresa winced when Philippe's lips touched the tender flesh.

"What's the matter?"

"Nothing," she said hastily. "I just stumbled and scraped my cheek, that's all."

150

"You're a terrible liar. I thought that something else was troubling you, but I wasn't sure of it. Come on, out with it." He drew her to him, playfully.

"It was nothing, really."

Philippe's fingers found the ripped seam of her bodice. "Don't tell me this is nothing. How did you tear your dress?"

Theresa tried to think of a story, but she could come up with nothing plausible. She had never been able to get away with lying to Philippe. Under his coaxing, she reluctantly told him, bit by bit, of her encounter with Julien St. Clair. In the darkness, she could feel Philippe stiffening with anger.

"Please, Philippe, I'm sure it won't happen again. I'll avoid him. It was foolish of me, and as much my fault as his."

"He took advantage of your misery. By God, the cad ought to be shot."

"But St. Clair is a powerful man! I beg you not to cross him!"

"Surely you don't think I'm simply going to let this go? You go on home. I've got a call to make." He began walking in the direction of St. Clair's home.

Theresa ran after him. "He'll kill you, Philippe!"

He shrugged her off. "Go on home. This is between him and me. Stay out of it."

She knew that once her husband had made up his mind, nothing would change it, so with a fearful heart she returned to her home. But tired as Theresa was, she would have no rest until Philippe returned.

The lights of the St. Clair house were ablaze as Philippe mounted the stairs, pushed his way roughly past the servant who met him at the door, and entered the drawing room. Julien, freshly dressed and bewigged and powdered, was sitting on a loveseat, entertaining Alphonse and Eugenie de la Houssaye. Despite his smarting cheek, he had already dismissed the afternoon's incident from his mind. He knew, of course, that women had to be wooed and that he had acted hastily; but he thought that a Cajun woman would be flattered by his advances and would have put up little resistance. Besides, the loss was really of no consequence.

Without a word, Philippe stalked into the room and pulled

151

Julien St. Clair off the loveseat with both hands. St. Clair's silk shirt was topped with a cravat that wound around his neck several times before cascading down his chest in a lace jabot. Grasping the stock, Philippe pulled it in both directions so that it choked St. Clair.

"If you ever lay a hand on my wife again, I'll kill you. Do you understand that, you miserable wretch?" He shook him back and forth, like a dog worrying a rat.

St. Clair, who was growing red in the face and choking so hard that he could not utter a word, tried in vain to speak.

"Do you understand me?" Philippe repeated, shaking him back and forth. St. Clair at last managed to nod feebly.

"Good." Philippe threw him roughly back onto his loveseat, turned, and without another word strode out of the room, down the front hall, and out into the night.

Julien St. Clair was speechless with shock and indignation. That he should have been accosted by such a miserable creature, and in front of two of the most prominent people in the area! In France, a man like Philippe Bernard would have been honored for his wife to receive the attentions of a nobleman. The outrage was too great to be borne.

He looked at his guests helplessly, and he saw the faintest shadow of a smile playing about the lips of Alphonse de la Houssaye. It was the final straw. *I'm going to kill that insolent beggar if it's the last thing I do*, he thought. *Philippe Bernard, your days are numbered*. He could not, of course, challenge him to a duel, as this would acknowledge Philippe as a gentleman and his equal. He would find another way.

As he entertained his guests, the wheels of St. Clair's mind were slowly turning, formulating the vague outlines of a plan of revenge. He was going to use Leon Landry to get rid of Philippe. Julien St. Clair knew that Leon Landry disliked Philippe Bernard. He did not know why, but he suspected that Leon was in love with Bernard's pretty wife. His instincts told him that there was, or had been, something between Leon and Theresa. In addition, Leon was a very ambitious man, and he, St. Clair, was in a position to help Leon in any number of ways. If he dropped a word in Leon's ear, let it be known that Leon stood to profit greatly by helping St. Clair rid himself of Philippe Bernard, he was sure that sooner or later the two of them would find a way. . . .

At home, Philippe told Theresa briefly what had transpired. "You must be mad," she said, clutching her throat. "He's a vain, evil man, Philippe, and you humiliated him in front of his guests. If you think he'll let it go, you're mistaken."

They undressed in silence and got into bed. She grasped Philippe's nightshirt in both of her hands and looked into his eyes, a look of pleading on her face. "Let's move west," she said. "You're right, I think we should go."

"I'm not going to run away because I'm afraid of St. Clair, Theresa," he warned.

"No, you're not running away. You brought it up before you even knew what he had done to me. I want to move. I think we should."

And so it was agreed that as soon as their crops were harvested in the fall they would move west, to the edge of the prairie country.

Chapter Eighteen

"Merde!" Philippe Bernard swore softly under his breath as he surveyed the ruins of his cornfield. The tender young stalks, so recently grown tall, lay trampled on the ground, ravaged by the hordes of wild cattle that had been a nuisance to the Acadians since their arrival in Louisiana. The Creole cattle barons had allowed their herds to roam at will, and despite the Acadians' protests that the wild cattle destroyed their crops and turned their own tame herds wild, the Creoles had refused to make any real attempts at control.

Two years earlier, the Bernards, Landrys, and a few other families, had left La Manque and moved west. Some of those who accompanied them were newly arrived in Acadia and had built no homes yet; others, like Leon and Philippe, were lured by larger land grants to the west or were beginning to feel hemmed in by the increasing number of families settling around the Poste des Attakapas. The group of settlers had stopped at the point where the bayou country met the open prairie and named the new community Landry, after its most distinguished inhabitant.

Soon after their arrival, the Acadians had elected their own representatives, or Sindics, to negotiate with the commandants of the Opelousas and Attakapas forts. One of their first concerns had been the control of wild cattle. The Sindics, led by Leon Landry, had finally persuaded Governor O'Reilly to issue an order that all cattle must be branded and penned during the growing season. But the Creoles refused to take action against each other, and nothing had been done. It was now more than a year later, and Philippe Bernard stood gazing angrily at his trampled field, seething with frustration.

"By God, I've had enough," he said to his neighbor Adam Armentor, whom he had invited to view the wreckage. The two of them turned and headed for Philippe's home.

"Perhaps we should consult Leon Landry," said Adam, trying to soothe his neighbor's anger.

"To hell with Leon Landry. He and his fine friends have done nothing but exact meaningless promises from the governor. I wouldn't give that for all of Governor O'Reilly's proclamations," he said, spitting contemptuously into the soil.

"The problem is that the commandants are always chosen from among the Creoles, and they always stick together and protect each other," said Adam, knitting his brows. "What good are laws if they're never enforced? Why doesn't the governor appoint one of our men commandant?" Adam's face brightened. "Why shouldn't you be commandant, Philippe? You'd have every cow in Acadia branded in no time."

Philippe grunted. "That will be the day. As far as the Creoles are concerned, we're the scum of the earth." In the years since Theresa and Philippe had left Maryland, Acadians had been flocking to Louisana from all thirteen of the English colonies, but although their numbers were steadily increasing, they could not compete with the Creoles, as the French people who had come directly from France were called, in wealth and influence.

"Someday they'll have to listen to us," Adam persisted. "There are more and more of us every day. You'd think the government would take our side once in a while—after all, we were invited to move here."

"We were invited down here because the Creoles needed slaves," Philippe said bitterly. "When that didn't work out, I don't think they were so happy to have us."

"What are you going to do?" Adam asked as they reached the Bernard house. The Acadians, remembering Philippe's expertise in smuggling in the old Acadia, knew him to be a man of action.

"Bullets, not words, are the only way to rid ourselves of these pests," said Philippe, running lightly up the steps of their home. He brushed past Theresa impatiently and took his musket from its place above the mantel.

Theresa paled and clutched his arm. "What's happened? You're not going to shoot anyone, are you, Philippe?"

Philippe laughed. "These are four-legged pests, Theresa, not the two-legged variety, although I've half a mind to shoot a few of the two-legged kind while I'm at it." He was collecting powder and shot and putting them into a brown leather pouch with the rest of his hunting gear.

Theresa had seen her husband cross the Creoles more than once, with never a thought for his own safety or that of his family, and she lived in constant fear that his impetuous nature would get them into serious trouble. "You can't go around shooting animals that belong to other people," she said.

"Just watch me." He stalked out the door.

She called after him. "Listen to me, Philippe. Your first responsibility is to protect your family. You can't go running off halfcocked every time you get angry. It's irresponsible!"

"If you wanted to be safe, you should have married another man. As for irresponsibility, your father warned you of that long before we married. You'll have to take me as I am, Theresa."

"At least ask Adam to go with you."

"That I will not. If there's going to be trouble, I don't want it to fall on anyone's head but my own." Philippe turned in the doorway. "Adam, please keep an eye on my family while I'm gone. I don't know how long I'll be away. If you need anything, Theresa, go to your Cousin Leon. I'll be home soon," said Philippe. "Don't worry."

"Oh, but I will," she whispered. "How can you do this?" She wiped a tear from her eye, then said a silent prayer as her husband ran down the stairs, his red hair gleaming in the summer sun. A chill ran down her spine, and she shuddered involuntarily as Philippe saddled his best horse, swung into the saddle, and rode away. The horse's hoofs kicked up a screen of dust as Philippe urged the animal to a gallop. Theresa put her hand over her eyes to shield them against the sun and strained to catch a last glimpse of horse and rider. When he left his home in anger, Theresa was always afraid that she might be looking for the last time at her handsome husband.

"What happened?" She turned to face Adam after Philippe had receded from view.

"Your corn was trampled by wild Creole cattle. Those people haven't done a thing about branding them."

"So it's wild cattle Philippe is after?"

Adam shrugged. He was relieved that Philippe had not asked him to accompany him. "I suppose so. One man alone can't do much against so many. But someone had to do it sooner or later."

"Yes, it's time something was done besides talk. But why does it always have to be Philippe?"

"Why not? Nobody else wants to court trouble, either."

"Yes, you're right." Theresa gave a short laugh, knowing herself to be inconsistent. All of the Acadians had been sitting around waiting for someone else to take action. No doubt other wives had persuaded their husbands not to risk endangering their homes by invoking the wrath of the Creoles.

She looked around her home, and her desire to feel that it was safe from the threats of her husband's fiery nature and the persecution of the Creoles expressed itself in a deep sigh. The more she had to lose, the more afraid she was of losing it.

Theresa cared for this home even more than the first one. It had been built with greater care and skill and was larger. The spot on which they chose to build was protected by two large chinaberry trees, which Theresa loved for the deep shade they provided and the lilac flowers they produced every spring. The new house, like the old one, was raised off the ground to prevent it from flooding, but the new one also had a separate room for cooking and eating. A steep roof jutted out over a railed porch. As in her first home, the inside walls were daubed with a mixture of mud and Spanish moss. A stairway on the front porch led upstairs to the sleeping attic.

Theresa loved the new land; in their new home, the last

vestiges of the strangeness she had felt when she first moved to Louisiana evaporated entirely. To the east, a bayou provided water; to the west, the rolling sea of prairie grass was broken by small round ponds around which grew wild lilies and fleur-de-lis. A large enclosure around each dwelling provided a pasture for the calves and horses, and a smaller one protected the flower and herb garden. Theresa was well known for her skill with herbs and medicine, and the beauty and variety of her new garden were her special pride. Two large cape jasmine plants flanked the brick walk leading to her home, as they had in La Manque. On either side grew roses and carnations, caracanthia and lilies, zinnias and marigolds. Wisteria and honeysuckle vines clung to the sides of the house. Her herb beds held those simple medicinals known to all Acadian housewives—mint and plantain, mustard, mamou and parsley, wild onion, anise, and a laurel tree—as well as the more exotic herbs she had brought with her from Maryland.

Theresa stood for a long moment surveying her domain after Philippe had left, then turned inside, shaking her head. She finished preparing a loaf of bread and crawfish stew for supper, then doused the small summer cooking fire. At the table, Jacqueline broke into her usual flood of chatter.

"Where's Papa?" she demanded.

"He's gone hunting," Theresa said quickly. "He said he might be gone for a few days."

Theresa presided over the rest of the meal in a fit of abstraction. She longed to be alone so that she could think. When the meal was over, she left the dishes to Jacqueline and went out to her herb garden. Safe among the plants she knew so well, she pulled up the weeds automatically, allowing her mind to wander as she worked. Philippe's words rang in her ears, stinging her. "If you wanted to be safe, you should have married another man. You'll have to take me as I am." Theresa frowned.

Since they had moved to Landry, Philippe had become increasingly headstrong. In Maryland, where they had been the humblest of servants, Philippe had accepted his lot cheerfully, finding release from the frustrations of life with his family. He had even swallowed his annoyance at Leon's

158

patronizing attitude, because he knew that he was lucky to have a job at all. Besides, Theresa recalled, their marriage was brand-new at the time, and Philippe's restlessness seemed to have been temporarily stilled.

After their move to Louisiana, Philippe had enjoyed the pride of ownership for the first time. He had worked hard to get settled, and had behaved himself until the incident with Julien St. Clair, which, Theresa had to admit, was more than justified on moral grounds. Fearful as she was of incurring the wrath of so powerful a man, she was secretly proud of Philippe for defending her.

After they had settled in Landry, Philippe's behavior had gradually become wilder, more erratic. The land itself was something of a liability. Except for the planting and harvesting seasons, during which he worked very hard, his energy was not fully occupied by his work. As soon as his crops were in, Philippe would meet with some of his neighbors and spend days at a time hunting or fishing, even when there were fences that needed mending or work to be done around the house. He had acquired a fast quarter horse that he loved to race, and he had even begun breeding fighting cocks, although Theresa disapproved heartily of the sport.

"It's not cruel," Philippe would try to reassure her. "Fighting is bred in 'em. It's natural. If you let two cocks go, they'll fly at each other and fight to the death without any encouragement. Nobody forces it."

Theresa remained unpersuaded. "It's not just the fighting. I don't like the drinking and gambling that go along with it."

"What's wrong with having a drink? And have I ever gambled away anything we really needed? No one can say that I don't provide for my family!"

This was true, but Theresa had had to reconcile herself to the fact that Philippe would never do more than provide a bare living. As soon as he had satisfied his family's basic needs, he quit working. "Life is too short not to be enjoyed," he would say with a wink. "What's the point of piling up money when you can't take it with you? Have you ever seen a corpse having a good time?"

Jacqueline adored him and would run to him for anything she wanted. It was Theresa who punished her when she misbehaved, and she grew tired, after a while, of playing the villain's part. Still, she knew that Philippe worshiped the ground she walked on. He remained physically faithful to her—of that she was certain—and he never drank to excess. An occasional gambling spree seemed to be his only real weakness, and his gambling never took food from the mouths of his family.

While Philippe could indulge his taste for hunting, fishing, and sporting, Theresa's work was never done. When she finished with the day's routine chores of feeding and washing, there were clothes to be cut from the yellow nankeen cotton she had spun and woven. There were sick people who needed her care. She would sit at night and rock on her porch, her body stiff with fatigue, trying to relax before she went in to bed. There were nights when she was too tired to sleep, and while she enjoyed the mild climate of Louisiana for most of the year, in the hottest months of the summer, the heat drained her strength.

Sometimes she would look across the wild grass nodding in the wind toward the large house Leon had built for Claudine and their children and shake her head, sighing. The house was painted with real paint; only the front wall of Theresa's house was even whitewashed. But Theresa noticed that Leon's pomposity grew with his wealth, and she imagined life with him unpleasant. Philippe's touch still melted Theresa as it had done in the old days, and although he exasperated her and she sometimes lost her temper with him, her love for him had only grown stronger with the years. Although Leon was unfailingly kind to Theresa and solicitous of her welfare and she knew she could always turn to him if she needed anything, in her heart of hearts, Theresa was not at all sure that she trusted him. For a while after she and Philippe had been reunited in Maryland, Theresa had agonized over whether or not Leon had lied to her when he told her that Philippe was dead. Communication in the colonies was so poor that it could well have been an honest mistake—Theresa had heard of other women who had married a second time, believing themselves to be widows, only to have their first husbands show up on the doorstep one day, so what had happened to her was not without precedent. After a while, she ceased worrying over it in her joy at having Philippe back, but there was always a nagging doubt in the back of her mind that Leon might be untrustworthy. She believed Leon to be content with Claudine and their family, and she thought that time had erased what he had once felt for her, but still, if Leon was capable of lying to her about Philippe's death, he might do something else like that in the future.

Leon was the only Acadian in Landry who had come from the colonies with any capital to speak of, and his efforts to increase his wealth were unceasing. Shortly after they had settled in Landry, he had purchased two slaves, a couple named Berta and Max. He had taken three steers to a New Orleans slave auction. An old trader accepted Leon's animals in return for two of his most "difficult" slaves. Leon looked at their sullen, undernourished faces and felt sure they would work out well on his property. They were, moreover, married, and although not young, they produced a male child not long after their arrival in Landry.

The night the baby came, Claudine had come running to Theresa's house, banging on the door breathlessly. "I hate to get you up in the middle of the night, but it's a breech birth, and no one knows how to turn a baby but you," she had said.

Theresa was up and dressed in minutes, following Claudine out into the night. In the cabin, the slave, Berta, lay moaning with pain. Theresa greased her small hands and turned the baby around so that it could come out head first, the way Pammy had taught her. Berta was barely conscious when the ordeal was over. "You have a fine boy," she said after she had washed the baby and handed it to its mother.

Berta stared at the dark infant, her eyes dulled. She whispered something Theresa could not hear. Theresa leaned over, smiling. No matter what the circumstances, no matter the pain endured, it always gave her a feeling of elation to help bring a child into the world.

"Berta, you have a healthy son," Theresa repeated.

"No," the woman whispered, a look of sadness on her face. "Massa Leon has a fine boy."

The bitterness with which she spoke brought back a vivid recollection of Pammy's face when she had told Theresa of her own child and the man who had been taken away from her. Theresa was appalled but could think of nothing to say. She patted Berta's hand. "You get some sleep now."

Back in the safety of her home, she had waked Philippe. "Philippe, I want you to promise me something," she said.

He shook his head, groggy with sleep. "What is it?"

"Promise me that we'll never own slaves."

"Are you mad? Do you know what slaves cost? I'll never make that kind of money."

"It's not the money. It's not right, and no good will come of it. Promise me."

"Very well, if it will make you happy, I promise. Now come to bed and get some sleep."

Each fall, after the harvest was in, Leon would take his extra cattle to New Orleans to sell. He drove them first to La Pointe, then over the Atchafalaya Basin to the Mississippi River and down the river to the city Theresa remembered with such fondness. He always returned with something for his house—a piece of furniture from France, silver candle sconces, once a linen tablecloth and napkins. Meanwhile, Claudine grew rounder and more complacent with each year and now had her breakfast served to her in bed by Berta.

Leon's industry kept pace with his wife's indolence. His latest experiment was a small stand of sugar cane. In the fall, when the cane was harvested, he showed Theresa and Philippe his crusher, a clumsy contrivance of two wheels, turned by mules. Berta's husband, Max, fed the cane stalk by stalk between the two wheels while the mules plodded in a slow circle. The juice ran down a gutter into a kettle that stood under a palm-roofed shed. "After you crush all the juice out of the cane, you boil it, and when it cools down, it makes sugar. You pack the sugar in bricks and ship it," Leon explained, unable to repress his excitement.

Philippe grunted. "I'm a cattleman."

"So am I," said Leon, puffing on his pipe in a self-satisfied way. "But I believe in diversification. No point in putting all your eggs into one basket."

"If you say so," Philippe muttered, lifting his eyebrows at Theresa.

She smiled back at him. There was no denying that Leon was very taken with himself. Although still young, Leon was already stout, while the years had hardly changed Philippe at all. He still had the body of a boy, lean hipped and hard muscled, and the hot sun of Louisiana kept his hair burned a bright red. Small lines about his eyes, caused by laughing and squinting at the sun, were the only signs of the passage of time Theresa could detect, and every time he came bounding up the steps of their home with his springing stride, she felt herself melt at the sight of him.

Still, there were the aggravations of his gambling and the somewhat haphazard way he maintained his farm. Only a few days before he ran off in search of the wild cattle, Philippe had bet their best milk cow on a horse race and lost it. Theresa had been stiff with anger since then, and when he fumbled for her in their bed that night, she had pushed his hands roughly away. It was the first time she had refused him, and it bothered her, but she thought that it would be even more insulting to play the martyr by giving her unwilling body to him.

Theresa rose from her herb bed and turned toward her house, wishing with all her heart that Philippe were back home. She felt a wave of desire as keen as those she had felt when she was sixteen and they had had to snatch clandestine moments with each other far from the prying eyes of her family. Suddenly, Theresa was sick with fear that he would not come back to her. She was deathly afraid of losing Philippe—her husband, her love, for whom she had risked everything.

She thought of her coldness to him since he had lost the cow—the stern look and tightly pressed lips with which she had greeted his shamefaced admission, the slow, dull anger that had burned within her since it had happened, the way she had turned her back to him in their bed at night. Guilt, so strong that she felt dizzy and nauseous, swept over her. She would never forgive herself if she never had the chance to let Philippe know that she accepted him just as he was. He did provide for her and Jacqueline far better than her father had predicted, and his vices, after all, were amiable ones. There was not a mean or ungenerous bone in his body.

Theresa walked up the steps onto her porch and sank

slowly into her rocking chair. She had been coldhearted and obstinate and unforgiving. What if God punished her by taking Philippe?

"Please," she whispered, "just send him home to me safe and sound, and I'll never complain again," she prayed. "Don't let anything happen to Philippe."

Chapter Nineteen

Theresa was never sure exactly what happened in the days that followed. The story of "Philippe Bernard and the Creole Cattle" was to become a favorite in Cajun folklore, and the tale grew with every telling. For generations to come, old men would tell their sons, "On the first day after Philippe Bernard left home, he slaughtered hundreds of wild cattle. They fell like rain before his bullets." Others felt the numbers were exaggerated. One thing was certain: wherever he went, Philippe left a trail of bloated carcasses to rot in the hot summer sun.

Theresa only knew that as the days dragged by, her anxiety for Philippe's welfare increased. After a week, she could no longer tolerate the waiting. She would appeal to Leon to go to La Manque for news. She did not like to ask him for favors, but she had nowhere else to turn. She collected Jacqueline, telling her only that they were going to visit their cousins, and headed for the Landry home. As she hurried down the almost imperceptible path that connected the two properties, she spied, in the stand of trees along the bayou, a single rider on a chestnut horse, who seemed to be gazing at her house. Her keen eyesight told her at once that he was not one of her neighbors, and the stillness and patience with which he sat led her to believe that he had been there for some time. As she progressed down the path, the rider turned and raked her with his eyes. The man made her uneasy, and she wanted to study him carefully so that she would be sure to recognize him if she saw him again, but something made her turn away from him, and her sunbonnet hid her face from his view.

About halfway between the two houses, she saw Berta running toward her. Therese knew at once from her haste and the expression on her face that something was amiss.

"Miz Bernard, thank God you come! You must have read my mind!"

"Whatever is wrong?" Theresa had never seen the black woman so agitated.

"It's my baby, Maxie. He's powerful sick, and nobody knows what it is. Massa said if anyone knew, you would."

Berta turned and accompanied Theresa to the cabin she shared with Max and Maxie, her rapid stride forcing Theresa almost to run to match her pace. Inside, Theresa sank to her knees beside the small boy, who lay on a pallet on the dirt floor. The stench of illness hung sickly sweet on the close air. The child was hot with fever and moaned when Theresa probed his flesh with gentle fingers. His lips were swollen and purple, his eyes bloodshot. Beneath his cotton shift, his back and chest were dotted with pustules.

"Does Maxie have a lump in the armpit?" Theresa asked Berta, who was hovering at the foot of bed.

"Why, yes, he does," she answered.

"And has he been vomiting?"

"Yes," she responded eagerly. "You know what it is, then?"

"I've seen it before, in Maryland, but only twice. Pammy, the woman who taught me most of what I know about medicine, called it African fever. She said only black people got it. I helped treat two slave children with it. But only Pammy knew the cure."

"Don't you remember it?" Berta exclaimed.

"I'm trying to." Theresa put her palms over her eyes and pressed, concentrating. It had been so long ago, and her mind was so full of her troubles. "I think I can make something for him, but I'll have to go home. You stay here. Keep cloths on

166

his forehead and try to keep him as cool as possible. I'll be back soon."

Theresa left Jacqueline with Claudine and trudged back toward her home, struggling to remember what it was that Pammy had given the two children. It would be easy to relieve the boy's symptoms. An infusion of dogwood leaves and twigs with sage, mint, and safflower would reduce his fever and vomiting. The skin eruptions could be eased with a mixture of ground dogwood with yellow dock and Solomon's seal root in hot lard. But there was something else Pammy had given them—she remembered that it had started with a decoction of squaw root and hawk weed. To this she had added yarrow and—was it dandelion or lobelia? There was one other ingredient, too. Sumac? Juniper? And what were the doses? It had been so long ago, and Thresa had so much on her mind right now, but she resolved to put aside her personal problems and think.

At home, she built a small fire, collected her herbs, and set several pots to simmer with what she believed were the right ingredients. On her way back to Leon's home, Theresa scanned the trees by the bayou as casually as she could. The rider on horseback had disappeared.

In Berta's cabin, the child was sleeping fitfully. Theresa held out the three jars she had carried. "The salve should be rubbed on the lumps. Keep a film of it on his skin. Give him a spoonful of this every hour for his vomiting. And this, I hope, is the cure for African fever. I'll be honest with you—I'm not sure I remembered it correctly. I don't know if this will cure Maxie, but I can assure you it won't hurt him."

Berta rubbed her son's chest and back with salve and woke him to administer his first dose of medicine. The child let out a thin wail and turned his face away, grimacing at the bitter potions. "I'll be with the Landrys if you need me," said Theresa. "I'll check back in a while."

Theresa was met at Leon's door by Claudine, swollen with her latest child. "Thank you for coming so fast," she said. "Berta's been out of her mind with worry. I'd have come for you myself if my delivery wasn't so close."

"I only hope I gave her the right medicine," Theresa replied. "The crisis should come in two or three days."

"You're more than welcome to stay with us if you can be away from home that long," Claudine said quickly. "We'd be so grateful. I was going to send for you, anyway, with the baby due any time. To tell the truth, I haven't been feeling at all well with this one. I've been so tired lately."

"Of course I'll stay, Claudine. Don't worry," replied Theresa, who had helped all Claudine's children into the world. "Hello, Leon," she said to her cousin, who had come out to greet her. "Could I speak to your husband a moment?" she asked Claudine.

Leon knew that Philippe had been gone for a week, and he had expected Theresa to turn to him for help, but he would not offer it. He had waited for her to come to him, wondering how long she would hold out. "I suppose you've come about Philippe," he said once his wife shut the door.

"Yes. I was on my way to see you when I met Berta. Leon, I'm worried to distraction. Have you heard anything?"

Leon knocked the ashes from his pipe and refilled it, savoring her distress. "I've heard rumors, but nothing definite. You know what he did, of course?"

"Yes, Yes . . . but Leon, he's been gone for a week now!"

"It was a foolish course of action. I've heard that they're shooting wild cattle in other places, too. Philippe seems to have set a bad example."

"Something had to be done. It's against the law to let cattle run loose during the growing season, but the Creoles won't enforce their own laws. We can't let them push us around forever."

"Patience, Theresa, time and patience," Leon said in his ponderous manner. "Nothing is gained by acting in the heat of anger."

Theresa refused to admit that she had said the same thing to her husband. "Whether he acted in anger or not, someone must defend our rights. We've been acting like a bunch of cowards, each waiting for the other one to come forward."

Leon sighed. "Philippe has turned it into a point of honor with the Creoles. Their pride is now at stake. But I won't argue with you, Theresa. You're a woman, and you just don't understand such matters."

168

Theresa repressed the sharp retort that sprang to her lips. "Yes, you're right, there's no point in arguing. I came to appeal to you for help."

"What exactly do you want me to do?"

"Go to La Manque. Talk to the commandant at the Poste des Attakapas. Find out what's happening."

"Perhaps I could do something for you. I do have some influence with the commandant."

"There's something else, Leon. Someone's been watching our house." She told him about the horse and rider she had seen by the bayou.

"I'm not surprised. If there's a warrant out for Philippe's arrest, the assumption would be that sooner or later he'll come home. That's why you're being watched."

"And that could be why Philippe hasn't come back. He could know they're lying in wait for him."

Leon nodded. "I'll look into it for you, but I can't leave Claudine until after the baby comes."

That very night, Claudine began to feel the now-familiar pains that began in her back. Theresa had just come back from visiting little Maxie, whose condition was unchanged, and was getting her daughter ready for bed. Leon knocked on the bedroom door and called, "Theresa? I think the baby's coming. Could you come in to see Claudine?"

Claudine lay propped up on pillows, her face pale but composed. Theresa patted her hand. "Don't worry about a thing. Just try to rest if you can."

Throughout the next day, Theresa went back and forth between Claudine's bedroom and Maxie's bedside. The boy's fever was beginning to subside, but it was too early to tell if her medicine had helped him. Claudine's baby was a long time in coming, and an anxious prick of doubt, which she tried to suppress, needled the back of Theresa's mind. By midday, Claudine was listless and her color bad. Her flock of children stayed outside, as they had been taught to do when their mother was having another baby, and Theresa cooked dinner for them so that Berta could stay by Maxie's side. She snatched an hour of sleep whenever she could.

Late the next afternoon, Claudine was delivered of a still-born baby girl. She cried weakly and helplessly as she stared at the small lifeless bundle. Theresa tried to remove the body, but Claudine insisted on holding it.

"You mustn't go on so," Theresa whispered gently. "I know it's hard to accept, but you've been so lucky to have other healthy children. I don't think I know of another woman who hasn't lost at least one." Claudine only turned her back and continued crying.

Theresa sent Leon in to console his wife and returned to the slave cabin. She knew that Maxie's illness would soon reach its crisis, and she was too worried about him to spare excess emotion for Claudine. His fever continued to drop, and the lumps seemed to be less sensitive, but that could be due to the other medicines she had prepared. Through the night, she and Berta took turns watching him, neither women getting more than a half hour nap.

The first rays of sun hit Theresa full in the face, and she stirred. She was sitting on the dirt floor of the cabin, her head resting against the door. Berta was stretched out on her bed, staring at the ceiling. Theresa's eyes went to Maxie, and she saw that his shift was wet clear through and clung to his back. Hastily, she turned him over on his back and felt limp with relief when she saw that his whole body was drenched in perspiration. His skin was cool to the touch, and beneath his shift the lumps had burst or subsided. She closed her eyes and whispered a small prayer of thanks. When she opened her eyes, she found the boy was awake and in his mother's arms.

"I'm hungry," he said.

Theresa smiled and touched his curly black hair. "Berta, your son needs some broth!"

"He's well," she said slowly. "It's a miracle. I was sure I was going to lose him."

She turned to Theresa, her eyes full of tears. "I'll be in your debt forever," she said. "I wish I had something to give you."

"Nonsense," said Theresa, remembering Berta's reaction to the birth of Maxie and touched by this display of maternal emotion. "You owe me nothing. You get Maxie something to eat while I look in on Mrs. Landry."

Claudine looked worse than she had the night before.

Theresa touched her forehead and was seriously alarmed at its heat. "What is it?" Leon ask anxiously, responding to Theresa's worried look.

Theresa put her fingers to her lips. "Outside," she whispered. "Don't wake her."

In the hall, Theresa said, "I'm afraid it's childbed fever."

"I looked in on her during the night, and she didn't seem to be mending, but I just thought she was unhappy over the child's death."

"No," said Theresa, shaking her head. "She's very ill, Leon."

"But Theresa, she's had her other children with so much less difficulty than most women. Why should this happen now?"

"I don't know—nobody knows what causes the fever. But childbearing is never safe. A woman can have any number of easy deliveries, and then. . . ." Her voice trailed off.

"She's not going to die, is she?"

"It's too early to tell. But there's no cure for this fever."

"You don't think Maxie's illness had anything to do with it, do you?" Leon's voice turned cold.

"No, I don't think so. Nobody knows the cause, Leon. She complained of feeling weak and ill before the baby came, so that could have lowered her resistance. We'll just have to wait it out."

For the next several hours, Claudine sank in and out of a delirious sleep, during which she tossed and muttered strange, disjointed sentences, most of them about her home and family in the old Acadia. She spoke of strange people Leon and Theresa did not know. "The snows are coming, Grandma," she said once, distinctly, with a smile on her face. And again: "Don't tease me so, Hector." She had occasional lucid moments, but she was growing weaker, and by nightfall Theresa took Leon aside and quietly told him to expect the worst.

Theresa's bedside vigil continued. She sponged her forehead and did her best to keep Claudine comfortable. Her breathing was so shallow that several times Theresa thought it had stopped. Around midnight, Claudine's eyelids fluttered, and she opened them. She smiled weakly at Theresa. "Take care of Leon for me, will you? He loves you so." She let out a long, ragged breath and died.

Theresa's tears flowed freely as she combed Claudine's hair and folded her hands on her breast. Then she went out to Leon. "It's over," she said quietly. "I'm sorry."

Leon was in the front room, disheveled and unshaven, sitting with his hands on his knees like a schoolboy. He nodded slowly. "She was a good woman, a good wife and mother. A good woman," he repeated lamely.

Theresa sat beside him and covered his hands with her own. "I want her to have a proper burial," Leon continued. "Father Verret is in La Manque and planned to come stay with us next week. If I went to get him tonight, perhaps he could come right away."

"I know that would be a great comfort to you, to have a requiem mass."

Leon rose to his feet heavily. "I know you did your best. Thank you for everything you've done for her and for little Maxie. I'll have to leave for La Manque at once, because of . . ." His voice trailed off.

"I know," said Theresa. "The heat. She has to be buried soon. I understand." She realized suddenly that she was bone weary, sick of illness and death and the burden of her own worries. She wanted to touch the walls of her own home, to be surrounded by her own familiar possessions.

"I think I'll be going home now. Berta can take care of the children, and I'm close by if she needs me."

"Of course. I'm sorry I kept you away from your own home so long. Give me a minute and I'll take you home."

"No, Leon, I'll walk. It will clear my head."

She expected him to protest, but he only nodded his head. "As you wish."

Theresa watched her cousin leave the room and wondered why he hadn't shed a tear for his dead wife.

Chapter Twenty

Throughout the following day, Theresa kept a watchful eye
toward the east, scanning the horizon along the bayou for
Leon's return and looking for the stranger on horseback.
After the evening meal, just before darkness fell, her patience
was rewarded by the sight of two men riding toward her. She
recognized Leon's wide figure and was sure the other rider
was Father Verret.

At dawn, Father Verret buried Claudine Landry with the
full rites of the Catholic church. In addition to Leon and his
children, Theresa and Josephine, four of their neighboring
families—the Armentors, the LeBlancs, the Trahans, and the
Moutons—were present. After the ceremony, Father Verret
took Theresa aside and said in a low voice, "I have some
news for you. Could I walk you home?"

"Of course, Father." Theresa could barely conceal her
impatience. The news must be of Philippe, she thought.

Along the path to her house, she stole occasional sidelong
glances at the man beside her, overcome once again by his
mysterious presence. Father Batiste grew rounder and redder,
his breathing more labored and his manner more officious,
every time Theresa saw him, but Father Verret had not changed
at all in the years she had known him. His body, lean and

elegant in his black cassock, seemed impervious to the heat, although his sallow skin was burned almost black by the summer sun. His cropped black hair and dark mournful eyes still lent him the air of aloof distinction that had always kept the Acadians at a respectful distance.

In her home, Theresa offered the priest a cool drink, and the most comfortable chair in the house. She kept her daughter busy gathering eggs in the barn.

"Have you heard anything of Philippe?"

"Yes. The commandant of the Poste des Attakapas has issued a warrant for his arrest. I don't mean to alarm you unnecessarily, but several prominent Creoles are considerably exercised over his slaying of their cattle. Julien St. Clair, in particular, is insisting on the harshest possible penalty." The priest glanced at her as he said this, and Theresa flushed.

"I had a long talk about the situation with Leon Landry on our way here. He tells me that you've seen the man who was sent to watch your house. Your husband is in hiding, at the moment, in La Pointe. He's being sheltered by a family named Benoit."

Theresa drew in her breath sharply. "You've seen him, then?"

"Yes. He's in good health and spirits, so don't worry about him. He won't be able to stay with the Benoits long, but the Acadians have rallied behind him, and I'm sure he'll find friends wherever he goes. He asked me to tell you that he'll come home as soon as he can."

"And when will that be?" Her voice sounded hopeful.

"I don't know. Leon will try to intercede on his behalf. It's not really fair to punish him for something all of the Acadians have wanted to do just because he was the only one with enough courage to act. I'm concerned, frankly, about the long-range effects this incident will have on relations between the Acadians and Creoles. I myself tried to talk Julien St. Clair into a more reasonable attitude, but he remains adamant and hostile on the subject of your husband. Has Philippe done anything to offend him?"

Theresa began fiddling with her glass. "Julien St. Clair

made improper advances to me, and Philippe barged into his home and threatened him in front of guests. The man was dreadfully humiliated.''

"I suspected as much. Do you know who the guests were?''

"Alphonse and Eugenie de la Houssaye.''

Father Verret shook his head. "Not good, not good at all. That explains a great deal.'' He sat silently, stroking his chin.

"What are we to do?''

"Just leave the matter in your cousin's hands for the time being. Leon is a skillful negotiator, the best the Acadians have. I'm sure we can reach a settlement of some sort. If I see Philippe again, do you have any message for him?''

"Just send him my love, and Jacqueline's, and tell him we are well and miss him. He's not to worry about us.''

"Very well. He said to tell you he'll try to keep you informed of his whereabouts. I've some other news, too, from your sister at Cabonnoce.''

"Claire? Oh, Father how is she?''

"She and her family are well, but I'm sorry to have to tell you that your mother died last month.''

"Oh.'' The priest sat silently while Theresa digested his mournful news. At last, she said, "I knew she was old, but I did so want her to see Jacqueline at least once. My little girl will never know her grandparents.'' Although saddened by the news, it did not affect Theresa nearly as much as the news of her father's death. "I wanted to visit Claire and my mother before we moved from La Manque, but my family couldn't get along without me, and travel is so hard.''

"I know it is difficult, but perhaps it is best that you remember your mother as she was in Grand Pré. Claire tells me that she was a vigorous and competent woman.''

"Oh, yes, she was wonderful. Was she so greatly changed when you knew her?''

He smiled. "I'm afraid so. She never really adjusted to the loss of her husband and her old home. During her last years, she was almost blind and very feeble. Her mind wandered, and much of the time she thought she was in the old Acadia.''

Theresa could hardly imagine her mother, always the busy housewife, as a senile old woman. "Perhaps you are right. Perhaps it is best that I remember her as she was.''

"I have good news as well. Your brother Claude and his family have arrived and are staying with Claire until the harvest is in. It's too late to clear and plant any land of his own. In the autumn, both families are thinking about moving to Landry."

"Claude and Claire are coming here?" Theresa was overjoyed. It was important that her brother and sister be nearby, especially now that their parents had passed away.

"It's not definite yet, but they have been trying to arrange it for some time now. Claire misses you very much, Theresa. With you and Claude and Leon, you could start a whole new community of Landrys right here."

"Oh, that would be wonderful. With so many of us, and our children, we would almost have the kind of family we had in the old days. Tell me about Claude. Who did he marry? How many children does he have? Why was he so long in coming to Louisiana?"

"Claude and René were sent to Massachusetts, but René ran away in the winter of 1763. There's been no word from him since. Claude married a girl from Port Royal and they had two children. He had finally saved the passage money to come to Louisiana when his wife fell ill. Her illness consumed most of their money before she died. Claude married a second time—a girl from Grand Pré. Do you remember a man named Joseph Melanson?"

"Why, yes, of course. He had six sons and a daughter named Denise."

"That's Claude's wife. It took a while for your brother to get together the money for his family's passage the second time, but they made it at last." The priest sat back and smiled. "Claire has another baby, a girl," he added.

"So much news! So they are really coming, in the fall, after the crops are in? Surely René will make it here one day."

He smiled at her eagerness, at the joy that suffused her face. "I hope so, for all your sakes. Claire wasn't sure whether you should be told about her move because it's not certain yet."

"I'll try not to count on it too much, so I won't be disappointed if it doesn't happen." They both laughed, know-

176

ing that she was already making plans and was filled with impatience to see her family and nieces and nephews.

Theresa had never heard Father Verret laugh before or seen him in such a relaxed, cheerful mood. "You know, Father, I've often wondered what you are doing working here," she blurted out impulsively. She blushed, regretting the words as soon as she had spoken them.

"What do you mean?" The priest looked surprised.

"Well, you are such an educated man, and it seems strange that you should be here instead of holding an important position at a European university. Everybody wonders about it."

"And what do people speculate?" he asked with a smile.

Theresa twisted her hands in her lap. She was in over her head, but it was too late to turn back now. "They say that perhaps you offended your superiors in some way and were banished." She cringed at her audacity, but Father Verret did not seem to take offense.

"I was banished, in a manner of speaking, but I did it myself. I asked to be sent here."

"Asked? But why?"

"Because I was arrogant and lacked charity. The simplest peasant with a loving heart would have gotten into heaven faster than I. 'What profiteth it if a man gain the world, and lose his soul?' There are more important things than book learning."

"And have you found them here?" she asked, genuinely concerned.

He drew his brows together. "Perhaps. At least I am trying."

Father Verret had always seemed to Theresa so cool, so aloof, so sure of himself. It startled her now to see the struggle he waged with himself beneath his self-assured exterior. He was, after all, just another troubled human being. She was surprised to realize it, and even more surprised that he had confided in her.

"Have you talked to anyone of these things?"

"No, for the simple reason that nobody asked. Besides, you are a sympathetic listener." Theresa lowered her eyes,

177

embarrassed at the compliment. He was not as complicated a man as he seemed, she thought.

"Well," the priest said, rising, "I have taken enough of your time. Is there anything I can do for you?"

"No, but thank you for the news you have brought. I feel much better now."

His thin lips curved into a smile. "I will bless Jacqueline on my way out."

Chapter Twenty-One

A week after Claudine's burial, Leon went to La Manque,
ostensibly to plead with the commandant on Philippe's behalf.
In fact, he went to confer with Julien St. Clair. "Our chance
has come at last," he told the haughty Creole.

Together they concocted a scheme for the final disposal of
Philippe Bernard. Julien St. Clair could never forgive the
humiliation he had received at Philippe's hands, and Leon
could never forgive him for winning Theresa. He had bowed
to the inevitable when Philippe had shown up in Maryland,
but he had never relinquished his ambition to own Theresa,
even after his marriage to Claudine. If his experience in the
colonies had taught him anything, it was the value of patience,
and he had been patiently waiting for years for his chance to
separate Theresa from the man she had had the audacity to
choose over himself. With the death of his wife, the last
impediment in his path was removed. There was no reason
now why he should not rid himself of Philippe Bernard once
and for all and marry Theresa. Philippe had conveniently
played into his hands by alienating the most powerful men in
his community.

While he was in La Manque, Leon did meet with the
commandant and pretended to make some attempt to dispose

him favorably toward Philippe, knowing that his efforts would be in vain. When he returned to Landry, he led Theresa to believe that he had made a serious effort on Philippe's behalf, but, he informed her, the news was not good.

"If Philippe's conduct is overlooked, it will set a dangerous precedent and encourage others to think that they may destroy property with impunity," Leon reported in his stolid fashion. He glanced around at his cousin's meager possessions and told himself how lucky she'd be to move into his own grand home.

"Then they mean to make an example of him?" she asked fearfully.

"I'm afraid so," he replied with a look that said, I told you Philippe Bernard would come to a bad end!

Aside from an occasional visit from a neighbor or from Leon, who dropped by regularly to check on the crops and livestock, Theresa and Jacqueline were left to themselves. Theresa felt lonely and pushed herself to work as hard as she could throughout the worst of the summer heat, grateful for any distraction.

One afternoon toward the end of July, she busied herself turning and beating her mattresses. Each bed had three of them, one of corn shucks, one of black moss, and one of feathers. Once every season she turned each mattress and beat it with a broomstick to eliminate lumps. She finished this task and served supper earlier than usual, grateful for the extra hour of quiet later in the evening.

She and Jacqueline were sitting on the porch when she was startled by the call of a whippoorwill. It was the signal Philippe had used to call her when they were courting in Grand Pré. Theresa looked up, searching the line of trees along the bayou, her eyes straining against the gathering darkness.

"What is it, Mama?" asked Jacqueline, always sensitive to her mother's moods.

"Hush!" she said, putting her fingers to her lips. "There it is again." A long, low whistle came from the east.

"It's your father. He's out there," Theresa cried, jumping up from her chair.

"Papa?" Jacqueline turned excitedly in the direction Theresa had indicated.

"Don't act as if anything unusual is happening, dear. He'll come to us when he's ready. Now listen to me." Theresa continued, once she calmed herself and Jacqueline. "Your father is going to visit us tonight." She held up her hand as Jacqueline jumped up and down with joy. "I know you're excited, but I want you to pretend you don't know. It's a secret."

Jacqueline immediately fell silent, confused over her mother's words.

"Come inside. I'll tell you a story."

Once they were settled, Theresa began. "There was an Indian who lived outside Grand Pré named Left Foot. Your father used to go hunting with him when he was a boy."

"What kind of Indian was he?" Jacqueline wanted to know.

"He belonged to the Micmac tribe, like most of the Indians around Grand Pré. One day, your father got lost in the woods. Night fell, and he was a little frightened. He had never spent the night away from home by himself before. He lay down beneath a willow tree and was trying to go to sleep when he heard an odd noise. . . ."

Theresa continued with her story, her ears straining for the sound of her husband's footsteps in the darkness. She had just gotten to the part in her story where Left Foot and his brother came out of the woods, revealing their practical joke to the frightened Philippe, when she heard a familiar step on the porch. In a moment, Philippe was in the room.

Jacqueline leaped up and threw her arms around her father's neck. Philippe hugged her affectionately, laughing and locking his arm around her neck. Freeing himself from her grasp at last, he drew Theresa to him and gave her a long, passionate kiss. Theresa clung to him, her face buried in his chest, grateful beyond all measure that her husband had been restored to her.

"Where have you been, Papa? Are you home for good?" Jacqueline clamored.

"Now hush. I can't answer all your questions at once." He

181

released Theresa and sat on the floor, his daughter before him. "Do you know what this is all about?" he asked.

"Yes, Papa, everyone is talking about you," piped Jacqueline. "You're a hero, and I love you!"

"Enough of heroics," said Philippe. He planted a kiss on his daughter's head. "The plain truth is that I've been skulking from one place to another like a common criminal on the run."

"Is it safe for you to come home now?" Jacqueline's face was aglow with the prospect of having her father home once again.

"No; it's not safe. I've got to leave tomorrow morning. I just couldn't stand not seeing you a minute longer. Don't ask me why I missed your funny face, but I suppose that proves a man can get used to anything." This was met with howls of protest from Jacqueline, who knew that her father thought her to be the most beautiful girl in the world.

Philippe's face became serious. "I haven't got much time. Theresa, how is the farm? Everything all right?"

"Oh, yes. Adam Armentor has been helping out, and Leon comes over all the time to check on us."

Philippe nodded. "And the cows that were coming down with pinkeye—they're all right?"

"Yes. We rubbed salt in their eyes, and it went right away."

"No problems with ticks?"

"No more so than usual."

"And the crops?"

"Fine. Leon says the cotton will be good this year."

Philippe nodded thoughtfully.

"When will it end?" Theresa asked at last, tired of Philippe's discussion of the farm trivia when she could think of nothing but the trouble he was in and how they were to return their lives to normal.

"I don't know," he said, letting out a sigh. "It's not over yet."

Their eyes met, locking, and a slow smile of conjugal complicity spread over their faces. The room and their daughter seemed to disappear, and there were only the two of them. When Philippe gave Theresa the special smile he reserved for her, the years melted away, and she was a young girl in Grand Pré again, being courted for the first time.

"Your father's tired," Theresa said to Jacqueline. "It's time for bed." She managed at length to silence her protests.

Theresa helped her daughter into bed, and at last she and Philippe were alone. Theresa removed Philippe's shirt and traced the lines of his collarbone with her finger. "I turned the mattresses today," she murmured.

"Aha! You must have known I was coming," he said in his usual teasing manner. She had missed his bantering jokes, his laughter, his touch, so much. . . .

She threw her arms around him, burying her face in his shoulder, amazed once again at the silky smoothness of his skin. "You've got to come home. I can't stand it any longer—the worry, the uncertainty, the waiting."

"You'll have to—just a while longer. Something's got to break soon. The longer they can't catch me, the worse it looks for them," Philippe said. He took her in his arms, smothering her with kisses. "This is what I really came home for."

"Philippe," she whispered. "Philippe."

He left before dawn, before Jacqueline was awake. Flashes of lightning, followed by the rumble of thunder, streaked the sky, illuminating his passage toward the bayou. The air was warm and heavy with rain. The storm broke just as he disappeared, sending sudden sheets of rain to pelt the house and the bowing, tossing trees. In the light provided by a brilliant streak of lightning, Theresa strained for a last glimpse of him, unmindful of her soaked nightgown.

Chapter Twenty-Two

Autumn and spring were the seasons Theresa loved most, although there was little autumn to speak of, at least not in the sense that she had known it in the old Acadia or even in Maryland. At first, she had thought that the season passed Louisiana by altogether. Then she had come to watch for the subtle shifts: the clear, pure air, with the sharp clarity of autumn; the bright blue sky; the gradual fading of the coarse prairie grass. Some of the trees changed. The leaves of the catalpa trees fell before the harvest, in September; after the harvest was in, usually with the first frost of November, the chinaberry trees turned a brilliant yellow, and soon after that the chinaberry leaves and berries fell, making a great mess that Jacqueline was cajoled into cleaning up.

That fall Theresa would have to see to the harvest herself, with the help her neighbors would give her. The cotton would be picked first, then the corn. Leon would let his own patch of sugar cane wait as long as possible, at least until the middle of October, as each cool fall day made the cane sweeter. Theresa knew that by All Saints' Day the crops would be in and the herds let loose over the shorn field. The hogs would root and grunt, gleaning cornfields and potato patches, and the cattle would move out to graze on the open prairie.

When harvest time arrived, Leon came by with Max, offering their help. "I can send Max and one of my boys to help, and Adam Armentor will lend a hand, too," Leon said. "I'm sure you've been wondering how to get everything done without Philippe." He called to Max over his shoulder to begin gathering wood for Theresa's home.

"Oh, thank you, Leon," Theresa replied. Then, feeling a rush of gratitude, she added, "I want you to know that I appreciate everything you've done for us. I don't know how we'd have managed without you."

"I'm always glad to help a neighbor and kinsman," Leon replied stiffly, but he flushed with pleasure like a young boy.

True to his word, Leon sent Max and Berta to Theresa's fields the next morning to help pick the cotton, and almost every day for two weeks one of his sons or Max arrived with the first light of day to assist with the harvest.

Except for Philippe's heroics, life went on as usual. Everyone in the small community of Landry knew that Adrienne LeBlanc had set her cap for Leon and meant to be the next Mrs. Landry. Old Mrs. Trahan died of the August heat, it was said. By harvest time, however, it became clear that Theresa was expecting a baby. For some people in Landry, that was news, for Philippe had been away for many months.

One mild morning, Theresa, in a rare moment of truancy from her duties, went for a walk along the bayou and passed Adrienne's mother, Camille LeBlanc.

"Good day to you, Camille. Has Espodie gotten in his corn?"

To her complete surprise, the woman turned away, shielding her tight little face with her sunbonnet. The unpleasant incident passed from Theresa's mind until the next day, when she spotted Jacqueline crying under the chinaberry tree.

"Whatever is the matter?" Theresa demanded. She crouched down and took the girl's hand in her own. "I don't want to talk about it," Jacqueline mumbled between her sobs.

"Come, Jacqueline," she replied, sitting down beside her. "You know we've never kept secrets."

The child hung her head. Theresa took Jacqueline's chin in

her hand and raised it, forcing their eyes to meet. "Tell me what's the matter. Has someone been speaking ill of your father?"

Jacqueline at last responded in a low voice. "It's not Papa they're talking about. It's you."

"Me?" Theresa was startled. "I've had time to do nothing but keep this place running!"

The child flushed scarlet. "It's the baby. There's been bad talk about the baby."

Theresa's limbs began shaking. "What kind of bad talk?" she asked gently. "Come along, child, out with it."

"Well," she stammered. "Uncle Leon's been spending some time here helping us since Papa went away. A lot of people think he's sweet on you, Mama. Now that Aunt Claudine is dead. . . ." Her voice trailed off.

"You can't be serious! They're saying the baby is Leon's? But that's absurd. Who would say such a thing?"

"The LeBlancs are saying it," Jacqueline volunteered at last. "Everyone knows that Adrienne LeBlanc is after Uncle Leon. The LeBlancs are saying that Leon won't marry her because of you."

"Did you tell them your father had been home?"

"Yes, but no one believes me." Jacqueline's tears flowed anew.

Theresa now had the explanation for Camille LeBlanc's silence. "And others must be saying these things, as well," she said to herself.

Theresa walked slowly to the porch and sat down in her rocker, where she took all of her troubles, and sat rocking back and forth, trying to decide how to still the rumors that were spreading. Five minutes later, she looked up to see Clement Aucoin.

"I can't stay long," he said. "I just wanted to tell you that Philippe was spotted by a patrol a couple of days ago. He didn't want you to worry about it, but he thought you might hear of it from someone else, so he wanted you to know that he's safe."

"Thank you, Clement."

Theresa walked her neighbor back down the road before returning home to prepare the noon meal.

The latest report from Philippe put the crowning touch on the new resolve that had been forming slowly in her mind. The next day, she visited Leon and told him of Philippe's latest escape. "How long can this continue?" she added. "He can't stay in hiding for the rest of his life. Something must be done. Please, Leon, talk to the commandant one more time."

He sighed. "I've talked before, and it hasn't done any good."

"But it certainly can't help his pride that Philippe has remained free for so long. This stalemate is no better for them than it is for us." She did not mention her other reason for wanting to hasten Philippe's return, but she assumed that Leon had heard the ugly rumors about the two of them.

"I can help you, but you've got to tell me where Philippe is." The plan he and St. Clair had concocted waited only for knowledge of his whereabouts.

"I'm sorry, Leon, but I gave him my solemn promise that I would inform no one of his whereabouts, not even you."

"I'll go into La Manque one last time and see if there's anything I can do. As soon as my cane is in, I'll make one last try."

True to his word, Leon came riding over one afternoon in early November. "I think we've reached a solution at last," he reported with obvious pleasure. "The commandant says that if Philippe will give himself up, he'll be given a light sentence to serve and then allowed to come home. That way the Creoles will save face, and it won't be too hard on Philippe. Julien St. Clair has been appointed to try and arrange a meeting with him."

"I don't think he'll ever give himself up, and certainly not to Julien St. Clair," she replied, aghast.

"He might as well be in prison now, Theresa. As you yourself said, this can't go on forever." Leon shrugged. "He'll just have to trust them."

"But what's to keep them from locking Philippe up for years? What, for that matter, is to keep them from hanging him?"

"Look, this situation is as much of an embarrassment for them as it is a difficulty for us."

"And the longer he evades capture, the angrier and more resentful they grow."

"Someone has got to break down this wall of distrust. Perhaps I could talk Philippe into it. Are you sure you won't tell me where he is now?" Leon asked casually.

"I can't tell you, Leon. I'd better go talk to him myself. If he won't listen to me, he won't listen to anybody."

"Very well, have it your way. But you'd better see him at once and try to set up a meeting before St. Clair changes his mind. He wants to meet him alone, in an open place. Both of them will be unarmed, of course."

"I'll talk to him and let you hear as soon as I can."

When Leon had left, Theresa sent Jacqueline to stay with neighbors, saddled Philippe's second-best horse, and set off at once. Her mind was made up to take action, and she was seized by impatience to complete her mission. She rode along the bayou, under the cover of its spreading oak trees, and then headed northwest, doubling back several times for fear that she was being followed.

She arrived a few hours later, tired but excited at the prospect of seeing Philippe, at the home of Robert and Ursule Thibodeaux. Robert roused Philippe at once, then excused himself. Philippe came out in his nightshirt. He folded Theresa in his arms and gave her a long, deep kiss. Smoothing her hair back from her forehead, he asked, "What's wrong? You shouldn't be traveling at this hour."

"Everything's fine at home. You're not to worry about that."

"The harvest?"

"It's just in. It was a bad time to leave, but I had to see you." She explained her errand.

Philippe shook his head. "Meet St. Clair? Unarmed? Come now, Theresa, I wasn't born yesterday."

"I don't trust him, either, but the only alternative is to give yourself up. This can't go on forever."

"I know. I've been thinking the same thing. I'd almost as soon go to prison as go indefinitely without seeing you. I'm ready to have the thing settled one way or the other. But—St. Clair!"

188

"He's a gentleman, Leon. Surely he wouldn't shoot you if you were unarmed."

Philippe snorted. "He may be a gentleman, but I'm not. When you're dealing with people who aren't bound by your code, you don't have to extend its protection to them. He wouldn't scruple to shoot a slave if it suited him, would he? We're not much better in his estimation."

"Leon has vouched for him. He apparently thinks St. Clair means you no harm."

"I don't trust Leon."

"Come now, Philippe, we've got to trust him."

"I'm not so sure. I've always been suspicious of that tale he told you in Maryland about my being dead. I think he made it up to get you to marry him."

"But surely he knew you'd come for me if you were still alive!"

"Yes, but the chances were good that I would be killed or that I'd be unable to get back to you."

"All kinds of stories floated up and down the river, and riverboat people aren't the most reliable in the world. You know as well as I do how they love tall tales and exaggerate everything they tell."

"Still, I don't see why anyone would have fabricated such a story. If Leon did make it up, it means that he would stop at nothing to get you. Now that Claudine is dead, there's only one thing to keep him from getting his way."

"I simply don't know what to say." Theresa shook her head. "The decision is yours, Philippe, but—there have been ugly rumors about Leon and me."

Philippe scowled fiercely, and she saw the muscles working in his clenched jaw when she told him of her encounter with Camille LeBlanc and the talk Jacqueline had heard.

"That settles it," he said, "I can't let you be subjected to such talk. That baby's mine and the world will know it!" He took two long strides across the room. He finally continued. "If I agree to a meeting with St. Clair, at least it will be a direct confrontation with one man. I think I'm better off taking my chances there. A man who would feel some compunction about killing in cold blood thinks somehow that justice has been done if he hauls you into court and has you sentenced unfairly. Something about a judge with a wig on his head and the drawn-out folderol that goes on in a courtroom, makes people think whatever happens there is all right."

Theresa came up behind her husband and took his hand. "What shall I tell Leon?"

"Tell him I'll meet St. Clair in the clearing three miles east of here, at sunset, day after tomorrow. Do you know the place I mean?"

"Yes. I'll tell him."

He patted her gently swelling belly and gave her a shadow of his old smile. "You'd better get some rest."

"No, I must get back. I may have been followed, and I don't want to leave Jacqueline overnight."

They walked out into the moonlight, and Philippe helped her into the saddle. She stooped over to kiss him good-bye. "Don't worry," he said. "I'll be home soon."

For the next two days, Theresa was grateful once again for all the work she had to do. On the afternoon of the day Philippe was supposed to meet St. Clair, Theresa was sitting with a sack of cotton, laboriously separating it from its seeds, when she saw Berta hurrying toward her. "Could I see you alone?" the black woman asked, looking over her shoulder.

"Why, of course. Come inside."

"I told Massa Leon I had to come get some of your itching salve. Before I forget it, you better give me some now. If he finds out the real reason I'm here, he'll kill me for sure."

"What's the matter?"

"Your husband is walking into a trap. I heard all about it."

Theresa's heart began thudding with a slow, painful beat. "What do you mean?"

The black woman twisted her hands. "I thought and thought about it. At first, I said to myself, don't get involved. It's not any of your business. But you saved my life, and you saved Maxie's life twice, and if I sit by and let this thing happen, I'll never forgive myself. It just ain't right."

"Tell me what you know. We haven't much time!"

"Either Julien St. Clair or Massa Leon plans to shoot

190

Philippe in cold blood tonight. They both hate him something powerful.''

''Are you sure Leon knows about this?''

''He's in on it. I'm sure of it.''

''But I have his word that St. Clair will be unarmed,'' Theresa cried. ''Why would Leon do a thing like that?''

''He'd do anything to get you to marry him. Now that his wife's dead, he figures with your husband out of the way, he can move right in.''

''I find that hard to believe, Berta. He was attached to me once, but that was so long ago. Surely these things don't last forever with no encouragement.''

The black woman shot her a knowing look. ''Lord, lord, you just like a baby. Everybody in Landry knows Massa Leon stuck on you something powerful and always has been. Even his wife knew it. Men like him are slow and patient, but when they want something, they don't give up until they get it.''

Theresa suddenly remembered Claudine's dying words to her. ''Take care of Leon. He loves you so.''

''Leon can't think I'd marry him after he conspired in my husband's death.''

''He'll swear he didn't know a thing about it. He'll say St. Clair lied to him, that he was deceived just as much as you were.''

''You're absolutely sure of this?''

Berta looked her in the eye. ''Would I be risking my life if I weren't?''

''Then there's no time to waste.'' She looked out the window at the sun. ''I'll just about have enough time if I leave at once.''

Theresa ran to her cupboard. ''Here's the salve—you go on home. I'll let you get a head start.''

When Berta left, Theresa took out Philippe's pistol with trembling hands. Thank God she knew how to use it. She gave her daughter specific instructions to stay inside with the door bolted.

Once again, she mounted Philippe's horse and forced herself to ride slowly until she had reached cover. God forgive me if I kill this child, she thought as she whipped the horse into a furious gallop.

Never had a trip seemed so long. She was riding a quarter horse, good for short bursts of speed but not a good distance runner, and she had to pace it to save it from exhaustion. The sun was sinking as she neared the clearing Philippe had named, terrified that she was too late. She tethered her horse at a distance far enough away so that she would not be heard as she approached on foot. At last, she reached the edge of the clearing. There, illuminated by the last rays of the sun, she saw Philippe, his hands held up in a gesture of surrender. Leon Landry, dressed in tight breeches and a flowing shirt with loose sleeves, in which he had undoubtedly concealed his weapon, stood sideways, sighting down the cocked barrel of a pistol. The black look on his hate-twisted face filled Theresa with such fear and loathing that she forgot her repugnance at the thought of killing a human being.

"You've made Theresa's life a misery with your irresponsible conduct, and you've never provided for her as you should," Leon was saying. "I'll be doing everyone a favor by shooting you. You're a lawbreaker and troublemaker."

"If you plan to murder me in cold blood, at least spare me your feeble rationalizations," Philippe replied. "But if you expect to win Theresa, you're mistaken. She's no fool, and she'll find out about this one way or another."

"You leave Theresa to me," Leon replied. "I'll convince her that you were shot by Julien St. Clair and that I knew nothing about it."

When Theresa spotted him lifting the gun, she aimed, fired, and watched in horrid fascination as Leon crumpled to the earth, a round neat hole in the side of his head.

Philippe ran toward her. "Theresa, thank God. I thought I was done for."

She stood staring at Leon's dead body, crumpled on the ground before her. "So much for honorable men," she whispered, her arm, holding the smoking pistol, hanging limp and slack at her side. She let Philippe hold her and kiss her gently.

"It's all over now," he said in a soothing voice. "It's all over."

Epilogue

Theresa was not present at Philippe's trial for the murder of Leon Landry. Women did not attend such affairs, and at any rate, she was concerned for her health. After her wild ride and the emotional shocks that attended it, she had found spots of blood on her clothing. She was dreadfully afraid that one more hard ride and another emotion-laden experience would cause her to miscarry. She heard, in bits and pieces, most of what transpired during the trial. Robert Thibodeaux testified that Philippe had been at his house throughout the evening in question; and Philippe himself solemnly swore, without perjuring himself, that he was not responsible for Leon Landry's death.

Not only was Philippe acquitted of the murder charge, but he had grown to be such a hero among the Acadians that it would have been dangerous to press charges for his destruction of the Creole cattle. The Acadians were by that time far and away a numerical majority in the region, and they had threatened the harshest reprisals if Philippe was imprisoned. Furthermore, emboldened by Philippe's success, the other brave Acadians had threatened to shoot any cattle that interfered with their crops or livestock in the future. The Creoles were at last forced to pen their cattle and begin behaving in a more responsible manner in their dealings with the Acadians.

Philippe Bernard returned to his home on a clear brilliant day at the end of November. The yard of his home was littered with leaves and berries from his two great chinaberry trees, and Jacqueline was convulsed with merriment at the antics of robins that were drunk from the chinaberries they had consumed. The birds wobbled around on spindly legs, unable to fly, and were so dizzy and disoriented that they were easily caught in their inebriated state by the little girl.

Philippe called out to Jacqueline. "Look at me, I'm as drunk as a robin!" he shouted, careening crazily about the yard. Jacqueline ran to her father and laughed until she was hoarse. Even Theresa could not suppress a smile. She was standing on her porch, smiling with fond indulgence at the foolishness of her husband. Their eyes met across the yard, and Philippe had her in his arms in an instant.

Two large carts, laden with children and household goods, came rumbling toward them. Upon seeing Theresa, a woman jumped down from the front cart and came running toward her.

"Theresa! Theresa!" she shouted.

"Claire!" Theresa flew down the steps and out of the gate as fast as she could. Philippe and Jacqueline turned to stare as the two women ran towards each other across the field, their arms outstretched. They embraced wildly, almost knocking each other over.

"Philippe!" Theresa shouted. "It's Claire!" Her husband joined them in a flash and hugged his sister-in-law. "And here is Claude!" she cried, turning to her brother in the second cart. Children jumped from the two carts and stood shyly under the scrutiny of Theresa, Philippe, and Jacqueline.

Claire, tears streaming down her face, turned to her brood. "These are your nieces and nephews, Theresa. Here is your namesake," she said, indicating a young blonde girl. "That's my husband, Roland with our baby, Claudette. These are my boys, Jean Baptiste and Germain."

Theresa introduced Jacqueline in turn to her new family. Then Claude introduced his wife and children. "Yes, I remember you from Grand Pré!" said Theresa to Claude's wife. "You were Denise Melanson then, Joseph Melanson's daughter. And, oh, you had so many brothers!"

"Six, and only the two women to look after them all," Denise replied with a smile. "I remember you, too."

"Did Father Verret tell you we were coming?" Claire asked. The adults settled comfortably on the porch, and the children played in the yard.

"Yes, and I dreamed of this day ever since. Were you able to get some land?"

"Just to the west of you. We'll be neighbors! I can't wait," said Claire. "We've got so much to tell each other! Remember when we used to stay up half the night talking after we got our own room, and Mama would come in and scold us?"

"Of course!" Theresa cried with joy. "We were so young then—nothing bothered us. But . . . what am I thinking of—you must be starving!"

That night, when their attic was packed with giggling children and Claire and Claude were settled in the extra bedroom with their spouses, Theresa and Philippe sat on the steps of their home, still too excited by the events of the day to think of sleep. Theresa inhaled the fragrant scent of woodsmoke and leaned her head on Philippe's shoulder with a sigh of contentment. For a long time, they sat in companionable silence, looking out over the land that belonged to them, and would belong to their children, and their children's children.

"What are you thinking?" Philippe asked at last, breaking the reverie.

"Do you remember the talk we had the night I found out my father was dead, before we left La Manque?"

Philippe nodded.

"You said that I had idealized the old Acadia in my mind, because I had been a child there, happy and protected," Theresa continued. "You said I thought we had been expelled from the garden of Eden but that it wasn't really as wonderful as I recalled."

"Yes, I remember. I said I liked it better here, and I thought we were going to be happier here than we ever would have been if we had stayed in Grand Pré."

"I thought you were wrong at the time, Philippe, but now I

agree with you. I do like the new Acadia better. I'm glad we were cast out of Eden."

Philippe caressed her shoulder, and she knew he was smiling at her in the darkness. "Yes," he said. "I imagine that Eden was a pretty boring place."

Acknowledgments

Many people have helped me write this book. For their advice, encouragement, and assistance, I would particularly like to thank Dr. Carl Brasseaux and Dr. Barry Ancelet of the University of Southwestern Louisiana's Center for Louisiana Studies. I owe a special debt to Dr. Brasseaux for allowing me to read the manuscript of his book *The Founding Of New Acadia* before its publication. I am also indebted to Margaret Kleinpeter for her research on the social history and medical practices in the colonies. Finally, special thanks to Steven Starsbury and Kathy Rodrigue for their assistance in typing the manuscript.

About The Author

Katherine Sargent is a pseudonym. The author lives in New Iberia, Louisiana, in the heart of Cajun country, and is married to a Cajun. Her previous novels are *The Triumph of Andrea* and *The Rose and the Sword*.